Jane and Her Fairy Friend to the Rescue

&

Other Stories

By

Nora Jean Broleman

Happy Duck Publishing
PO Box 607
Belle, MO 65013

Genre: Fiction, General
ISBN: 978-0-578-66921-2
First Edition.

Dedicated to my husband Jack and our daughter Jodie

Many thanks to the many people that have helped; especially my husband, our daughter, my editors, and publisher.

CONTENTS

Jane and Her Fairy Friend to the Rescue

I come to a sudden stop in the middle of the gravel road, two miles from my new house. A good distance away I see a man and a woman with their hands raised in front of two other men.

Assuming they are being robbed I yell, "Hey!"

At the same time I hear two gunshots and see the couple slump to the ground.

One of the men turns to point at me. I spin to the left and with Buffy, my standard poodle, at my heels race into the woods while hearing the slap of a bullet in the leaves above me.

Dodging trees and bushes we run until knives of pain slice up my sides as I gasp for breath. I stagger to a stop, bending over; gulping air through my open mouth. Buffy sits beside me. Raising my trembling arm over my head signals her to lie down. My hand drops to pat her head as I gasp out, "Good girl." I collapse to the ground beside her.

Trying not to cry, I bury my head into her soft hair. "You are so wonderful," I coo to her.

I'm shaking. I tell myself I just need a couple of minutes to rest and listen. Nothing. I can't even hear a bird singing. I feel sure I was too far away for them to identify me since I hadn't seen them well either. They won't know which way we were running. I doubt they are dressed for the rugged Missouri terrain as well as I am.

The cottage I recently inherited from my Grandmother backs into Missouri Department of Conservation woods. The road runs along the edge of their woods. From the map I'd looked at, the forest stretches out a long ways. Looking around, the woods appear the same in all directions. I sigh while struggling to my feet, picking what I hope is the direction toward home. "Come on, Buffy. Let's go home."

About an hour later, I know we are lost. Taking my water bottle out of my backpack I drink half, and then pour the rest into Buffy's dish. Exhausted, I sit on a fallen log; talking to Buffy for comfort while petting her. I go over what I witnessed. The two men must have shot the man and woman. My first guess was robbery, but I don't know. Since the one took a shot at me I am certain they'll kill me if they can find me.

Tugging slightly on Buffy's leash, we get up. Since the way we'd been going isn't the way home, perhaps I should try to find my way back to the road. Which way? I pick one and we start jogging again as I slap the insects, brush, and branches away from me bloodying my hands.

Startled, I stand still at hearing a slight noise. It sounds like feet coming toward me. Don't panic, I keep saying to myself. Giving Buffy the down signal, we crouch behind some bushes. The sound of rustling leaves being stepped on comes closer.

With trembling hands and heart pounding, my eyes dart around trying to see those men. I'm sure they must be tracking me. Holding on to Buffy's collar, I unsnap the leash. If I am shot, I love her so much I want her to be able to run away.

Wrong, wrong, wrong! How stupid of me. She won't leave me. Maybe she'll attack them to protect me.

Wrong, wrong, wrong! She is a poodle and has only growled once at a human; the guy in St. Louis who was flirting with me.

A beautiful doe deer materializes in front of me prancing with her two fawns, jumping and playing. Sighing with relief, I clip the leash back onto Buffy's collar as her tail begins to wag slowly. Sensing us, the doe's tail raises like a waving white flag as they bound swiftly away. I sit there laughing nervously, petting Buffy as some of my tension eases up.

The darkening sky confuses me. Have I been running around in circles for a solid day? Stupid girl, I think to myself. I have a watch I haven't thought to look at until now. It is six p.m. The lack of sunshine and cloud cover hint at the coming of rain. We've had nothing to eat all day. My stomach hurts, my body aches from tripping and falling. Plus, we are out of water. Don't panic, I keep repeating. We are lost, but don't panic!

We trudge on for another hour when, in a rocky area ahead, I spot what might be the opening to a cave. Being the brave female I am; I remove the leash from Buffy's collar sending her in to search. A minute later she comes back out, sitting in front of me showing no concern.

Taking my small flashlight from my backpack, I bend over; crawling inside the opening. It is only about a four by six foot hole and not tall enough to stand up in, but it will do for the night. Feeling grateful to be safe from rain, I sit down and start rummaging through my backpack, hoping for anything edible. Yea! I find a small bag of Buffy's kibble. I dump it into her dish. She sits patiently waiting for me to say "Okay" before she starts eating.

There is nothing for me. I consider chewing on some of Buffy's kibble, but she makes short work of it. In a way, I'm glad I hadn't had to make the decision to eat it. I sit petting her for a few minutes after she finishes eating, more for my comfort than hers. I sweep small rocks

from the ground with my hand. Then I use
my shirt to wipe blood, dirt, and sweat from
my face. Laying down I use my jacket for
cover. Buffy curls up against me. The sounds
of whip-poor-wills and katydids feel
comforting. I figure they'll shut up if someone
is coming.

I am startled awake with my heart
pounding, seeing the sky start to lighten;
amazed I'd slept all night. My stomach growls
from hunger as we leave the tiny cave and
start walking briskly. I carry Buffy's leash, but
don't connect it. We aren't running. I know
she'll stay near me. I'm feeling a tad bit
calmer this morning. I start noticing the
beauty of the wooded area where we are.
There are wild flowers and green trees
everywhere. I smile to myself knowing I could
enjoy these woods if I weren't lost and
hungry.

Several hours later I am wondering if I
should yell for help, but don't want those two
men to hear me. Good decision, I decide as I
soon hear water running. I am so thirsty. I
know I'm going to drink it, even if it makes
me sick. We walk a little faster. Just as I see

the stream Buffy surges ahead and I hear her loud lapping noises.

Taking the empty bottle from my backpack, I drop to the ground beside the stream and lower the bottle into the ice cold water. It must be a spring fed creek and might be safe for drinking. I drink the entire bottle and refill it. Now we have water.

Slowly raising my aching body I lead Buffy along the side of the rippling creek, hoping it will lead to civilization. Besides, the sound of it is pleasant. There are pretty rocks and tiny fish in the water, plus lovely flowers at the edge.

Between the holes and fallen branches that keep tripping me, my legs and feet ache even more. No one's following me. It feels as though my stomach is trying to eat me. The creek keeps running along. I'm beginning to think, when I'm not dreaming of food, that it will go the entire length of this forest without crossing a road or going near a house. It's getting dark again. I refuse to feel despair.

Finding the cave was great last night, but I can't see any likely place now. The holes are big enough for a woodchuck. Not even Buffy would fit in one. I toss some fallen leaves up against a larger, rotting log and lie down pulling Buffy up against me.

Focusing on the good news that no one is following us, I try to go to sleep. The hard ground, chilly air, and empty stomach won't be ignored. Before I can stop myself, I'm hugging Buffy while crying. Okay, I admit to myself, I am feeling despair.

Sitting up hugging my knees, I start wishing I had something to use as a weapon. A flash of blue and white is fluttering with a wisp of sound before my eyes. I swipe at something as I feel a slight touch on my cheek.

Buffy sits up showing no concern. She is tilting her head as though she is curious.

The moon comes out from behind a cloud giving me enough light to see whatever this is. I have obviously lost my mind because I'm seeing something which can't be real. It looks like a beautiful small fairy from a children's book. I blink. I still see her short gauzy wings which appear to be made of flower petals. She has small, pointed ears. Her sparkling white dress is under a billowing royal blue cloak with numerous dangling pink ribbons. Her feet are bare as she hovers about two feet from me at eye level.

I laugh, no longer afraid, knowing it is a hallucination; probably from lack of food.

"My name is Taylor. I'm a real live fairy you don't believe really exists." She pauses, perhaps waiting for me to reply. My mouth hangs open, but I can't utter a sound, only stare.

Taylor smiles. "That's okay. Please don't be alarmed. I stopped to see if I can be of assistance to you and your dog. She is a standard poodle, is she not?" Another pause. This time I manage to nod.

"What's her name?"

"Buffy," I manage to squeak.

"Hi Buffy. May I come near you?"

Buffy's tail beats a tattoo on the ground becoming a drum roll as Taylor comes quite close and appears to kiss her.

Taylor hovers in front of me. "What is your name, my dear?" she asks in her beautiful, tingly voice.

"Jane," I whisper. I must still be asleep and dreaming, a silly, silly dream.

Taylor smiles, "Well, Jane, consider me your friend. Please tell me if you want to go home and where home is. I'll see what I can do."

I decide to go with the flow of this dream to see what happens. "Taylor, I witnessed a murder. If they find me, I'm sure they will try to kill me. I don't think I was close enough for them to know what I look like or who I am because I couldn't see them very well."

"Alright then, what do you want me to do?" Taylor's smile widens as though she is delighted with my predicament.

"Take us home, I guess." I'm annoyed with her excitement and hoping I am still asleep or else my mind has flown away like a cloud. "I have a small cottage inherited from my grandmother on Dry Creek Road at the edge of the woods."

I blurt out before Taylor can say anything, "Buffy has only had a bit of kibble and I've had nothing to eat for two days."

"Piece of cake," Taylor says. With the nod of her head, a chair appears beside a small table covered with grapes, cheese, crackers and a bottle of water. Buffy's drum roll with her tail makes me look down and I see a large meaty bone in front of her.

Buffy looks up at me yipping and wiggling, her tail going ninety miles an hour. She knows she can't eat it without my permission.

"Okay," I say. Buffy is tearing chunks of meat off the bone before my mouth closes.

Taylor beckons me to sit. She lands on the edge of the table opposite the chair.

Without further invitation, yet still assuming I am dreaming, I sit gobbling up the sweet, juicy grapes. Every bite of the Cheddar and Swiss cheeses are wonderful. I feel so full. I am beginning to doubt I could feel this way in a dream. I share the bottle of the water with Buffy and am shocked to see it is full again when I set it down. Grinning, I apologize after my slight burp.

Buffy is still chewing on her bone, but is now lying on a beautiful Oriental rug. Where did this come from? Woven in bright purples and reds, it must be worth a fortune. Taylor softly asks me to sit on the rug in back of Buffy, holding on to her.

Having no idea why, I obey; noticing the table, chair, and bottle of water have disappeared. As Taylor sits down in front of Buffy, we start rising off the ground. I laugh out loud. Why not a flying carpet? The moonlight allows me to watch the wooded area as the carpet winds between trees and up into the sky. It levels off, skimming over trees and hills.

The breeze races by us like a train going in the opposite direction. My hair whips around as though we were in a convertible on a highway. Buffy shows no sign of concern holding her bone securely in her mouth, but I hold on to her even tighter. In less than thirty minutes the carpet slows down. I look at my watch. It is almost midnight.

In the darkness the gravel road we are approaching is a ribbon of lighter color running through the blackness below. Feeling disbelief I think I recognize Dry Creek Road where my cottage is located. Buffy and I had walked all day today and ran most of yesterday, all of it in the wrong direction. There is no way we could have covered the distance back to my house in such a short amount of time. I know we were lost in the woods but hate to believe we were that lost.

"Which way?" Taylor asks.

"Left," I reply feeling nervous, my thoughts filled with questions. Could this be real? Is it just a dream? "We better get off here, so no one will see us."

"Not a problem," Taylor giggles. "No one can see us because we are invisible."

"Of course we are," I whisper. "If we can be on a flying carpet, we can certainly be invisible."

"Is it the little blue house next to a reddish wood barn?" asks Taylor.

"Yes," I shake my head dazedly as the carpet lands us at my front door. Taking my key out of my pocket, I giggle. "Thanks for the food and the ride home. I'll look for you in my next dream."

Buffy and I walk into the house. I put some kibble and fresh water in her dishes. The warm shower is heavenly. Quickly drying off, I pull on my nightgown and fall into bed for what is left of the night.

Sometime the next morning I roll over mumbling, "Umm I smell coffee, Buffy." No Buffy. I jerk awake, sit up, staring around me. My bedroom door is still closed, but Buffy is no longer in the room. Smart as she is, I know Buffy can't open the bedroom door or make coffee. Someone had been, or still was, in my house.

I know I have the only key to my house. There are no relatives or friends nearby. Panic rises up my throat beating at my brain. Have those two men found out where I live? Why didn't they kill me? Throwing on my robe, I grab my small Sig Sauer pistol from the bedside cabinet, and then slip into my slippers. Walking to the door, I hear nothing.

Turning the door handle slowly and quietly with my shaking hand, I step into the hall. No one there.

I creep toward the kitchen and peek in the door. No one there. Next I come to the door to the living room. No one there. Panic flares up my throat again. Where is my wonderful dog? Have they hurt her?

I collapse onto the couch. The front door starts to open. My mouth hangs open. My breath catches in my throat. I raise the pistol pointing it to the opening door.

Buffy bounds into the room tail wagging, Taylor on her back. "Whew," my breath blows out as I lower the pistol, putting the safety back on.

"Sorry if I scared you, love," says Taylor smiling. "Have you had your coffee?"

My heart is still pounding, making it hard to hear. My hands shake. I draw some deep breaths trying to calm down. "No," I finally manage to whisper.

"Well, come into the kitchen, dear. You'll feel better after drinking some coffee."

I totter after Taylor and Buffy feeling my legs steady as I walk.

"I've fed Buffy and we went for a walk."

"Waaa," is the only sound coming from my mouth.

Taylor flies to my shoulder brushing her tiny hand on my cheek. I can barely feel it, but it calms me completely. "Thanks," I mutter sitting on a kitchen chair. "I'm fine now." A cup of coffee appears in front of me.

"Do you take milk or sugar?" Taylor asks.

I shake my head, taking a sip. Liquid heat flows down through my chest into my stomach. I am awake now. "Thanks," I say again, feeling my head starting to clear. I look around, noticing my kitchen seems cleaner than before. That pesky spider web in the ceiling is gone. "You cleaned my kitchen?"

"It was already clean. I dusted a bit." Taylor smiled. "After breakfast, what shall we do today?"

"We?"

"Sure. If it's alright with you, I'm going to stay with you for a while. I want to make sure those men you mentioned last night won't be trying to hurt you."

Sounding a little daft I say, "You're going to stay with me?"

"Certainly," Taylor smiled again.

Taylor smiles a lot, I notice. She is a very real, beautiful, tiny fairy. I smile back at her, glad my fairy friend will stay with me. "I'll fix breakfast, Taylor. What would you like to have?"

"Don't bother. It's much faster if I do it. What will you have?"

Buffy looks up at me as I laugh out loud, and then puts her head back on her paws to continue her nap. "Crisp bacon, two eggs over medium, and a biscuit with butter and strawberry jam."

Only slightly surprised, I survey the plate that appears in front of me. Exactly what I ordered is on it; along with knife, fork, and glass of orange juice. I grin, digging in while noticing a fairy sized table and chair at the other end of the table with a plate of fruit for Taylor. We eat. The dirty dishes disappear.

"Thanks. I could get used to this."

"Don't," is Taylor's snappy come-back. "I might let you cook and clean up next time. Back to my earlier question: what shall we do today?"

I think for a second, trying to decide. "First thing I want to check my computer or buy a newspaper to see what happened to the two people I saw shot. It's Monday. I work from home typing medical transcriptions. What about you? Is there anything you need to do?"

"Nothing. Go check the computer for that information. If you need one, I'll get the newspaper. And show me about typing medical transcriptions. I'll see if I can help."

A few minutes later, Taylor hovering over my shoulder, we read the sheriff's report about a Mr. and Mrs. William McDonald killed with single shots to the head. No leads at this time who committed the murders or why. I know I should call the sheriff to report what I'd seen. But I hadn't seen enough to help them. I was too far away. Besides, reporting it might lead those men to me. Guilt tries to make me change my mind, but I convince myself to play it safe. Anyway, I need to start typing those medical transcriptions and sending them off before I get behind. I put the headphones on over my ears, drowning out the guilt as I listen and type.

Taylor swoops down in front of my face waving her arms. I stop the machine and take off the headphones.

"Come quick!" says Taylor. "Two men just got out of an automobile in front of the house. Sit down on the rug behind Buffy."

"They could be anyone. I want to peek out the window at them."

Two men are standing by a faded red sedan talking. They are vaguely familiar.

"I wonder what they're saying."

Taylor smiles slightly. "Do you have those religious tracts?" booms a man's voice.

I jump.

"Yeah. Are you sure this is the right house?"

"The boss said a single woman with a poodle live here. That's who we saw. We get rid of her; we get rid of the only witness and evidence against us."

"What if she's not home? The place looks empty."

"We'll hide in the car and wait. You take the religious tracts while I look for a back door."

"Okay, Taylor," I say. "Let's get out of here." I race into the kitchen and sit down behind Buffy on the rug. Taylor flits onto the rug in front of her. The rug rises, the door opens, and we're off. I think I see the door close and one of the men starting around the corner of the house, but I know Taylor has made us invisible.

Worry gnaws at me. Someone tracked me down. I don't know who. The rug is flying toward town and settles down a block from the sheriff's office. Buffy and I stand up and walk off the rug. We can't see it anymore. I set off for the office with Buffy beside me.

"Hi," I say to the officer sitting behind the glass windows over the counter. "My name is Jane Unger. I live on Dry Creek Road. I flew out my back door, got a ride here because I think the two men who were coming up the walk to my house intended to kill me. They are probably the two men I think I saw kill Mr. and Mrs. McDonald." I pause. The officer had straightened up giving me his full attention.

Glancing at Buffy, the officer says, "Please take a seat in the waiting room. Someone will be out to speak with you in a minute."

Almost before I settle into one of the uncomfortable plastic chairs, the door opens and two officers enter the waiting room. One is the officer who had been at the desk. I notice someone else is sitting there now.

"I'm Sheriff Jerry Baxter," says the younger officer who is very good looking with a confident smile. "This is Deputy John Miller. Let's go back to a conference room to talk."

I follow Deputy Miller through the door with the sheriff following me. We go in a larger room with a table surrounded by chairs filing the center of it.

"Ms. Unger," says Deputy Miller. "Please sit down so we can talk. Your poodle is certainly well trained. Do either of you want something to drink?"

"Please call me Jane. We're fine." I signal buffy to lie down beside my chair.

"Jane, then," says Sheriff Baxter. "Please explain why you think those two men want to kill you."

"Yes, sir, of course," I answer politely. "While I'm explaining, could you please send someone to my house before they do too much damage there?"

Deputy Miller stands up. "What's the address?" I tell him and he goes out to the office. A few minutes later he returns with a tape recorder. "Is it alright if we tape your statement?"

I nod.

Deputy Miller turns on the tape recorder, identifying the date, time, our names, and that I have given permission for the recording. "Jane, would you give your name and permission?"

"Yes, sir," I speak slowly and clearly, feeling very nervous. "My name is Jane Unger and I give permission for this recording."

"Thank you," says Sheriff Baxter smiling. "Please tell us why you are here and why you think someone intends to kill you."

I smile slightly and begin with seeing the couple with their hands raised. "Did you recognize the couple or the men?" asks the sheriff. I continue, explaining I was too far away, being shot at and racing into the woods. I admit to being lost in the woods with Buffy until Sunday night and getting home about midnight. Taylor is left out.

"That brings me to now," I say. "Two men came to my house, I heard them say I was a witness and was afraid so I fled and came here."

Deputy Miller turns off the recorder. He and Sheriff Baxter look at me for a minute. Sheriff Baxter asks "Jane, do you have someone you could stay with for a while?"

"Not really," I said doubtfully. "May I just hang out here until you pick up those men?"

Officer Miller takes the recorder out of the room.

"You need to wait to look over and sign the typed statement from the recording. After that you may sit here as long as the room isn't needed or stay out in the waiting area," says Sheriff Baxter. "I'll come tell you as soon as we know anything."

Deputy Miller brings me a glass of water. I settle back with a magazine. Thirty minutes go by.

"Jane," says Sheriff Baxter giving a sheet of paper to Deputy Miller and walking over to me. "You were right to get away from your house. Two men ran out and off into the woods when a deputy pulled up. He didn't find them or their vehicle. I'll take you home now so you can check for anything missing."

"Ohhhh," is all I manage while reaching down to pet Buffy's head, thinking about how bad this is and what I am going to do.

"Jane," says Sheriff Baxter softly, stepping closer to me, placing his hand on my shoulder. "The deputies didn't see the men enough to identify them. They are white, about six feet tall, and not heavy. It isn't much to go on."

I find I'm holding my breath and start breathing again.

"Let's go to your house now. You can stay there, but it's obviously not safe for you. I suggest you pack a few belongings, then drive yourself somewhere safe. Please call, giving us your new location."

I rise feeling slightly numb with fear, yet grateful I wasn't shaking. Two days lost in the woods and now this. "Thanks. That's good advice. I'll let you know where I go."

When we get to my house, Sheriff Baxter escorts me to the house leaving me on the porch while he checks the rooms inside. "No one seems to be here. Will you check to see if anything is missing?"

I walk through the house. Nothing seems to be touched. I go back to where the sheriff is standing to tell him.

Sheriff Baxter takes a card from his pocket, writes his cell phone number on the back and hands it to me. He gives me a big smile making me notice again how good looking he is.

"Thanks, Sheriff Baxter."

"Please call me Jerry. Phone me anytime day or night, if I can be of help. You should find somewhere else to stay for a few days."

"Thanks again, Sheriff, uh, Jerry. I appreciate your help. I'll let you know when I get settled somewhere." I find I'm smiling shyly at him ignoring the butterflies in my stomach.

"My pleasure," says the sheriff turning toward the door. "Be sure to lock up."

Locking the front door, I go to the back door to check if it is locked. Collapsing on the couch, I pat the cushion for Buffy to join me. She does. Petting her helps keep me calm, but my head is full of questions. Where can I go? How can I get my typing done and send it off if I'm not here? How will I get more transcriptions to type? I can't afford to stay in a motel. Even if I could, they probably don't allow pets. I need coffee and food. I haven't had enough sleep. I'm tired. I think about getting up.

"Hi Jane," comes Taylor's sweet voice as she flutters into the living room.

"Have you been in the house all this time?" I blurt out.

"No, dear. I was here for a while. Then I stayed nearby in the woods. By the way, I finished your typing, but wasn't sure where to send it. Why don't you do that, then come to the kitchen for fresh coffee and a fruit salad?"

I know I look stupid with my mouth hanging open, I certainly feel that way. "You are so tiny. How could you possibly type?"

"Jane, dear," she giggles. "You are correct. I don't actually type with my fingers. After listening to the recording, I told the machine to type. There is practically no limit to my magic. I just have to think what I want to happen and it does. Kinda' cool, right?"

"Yeah, real cool, Taylor." I laugh as I stand up and go to the computer. After sending off the transcriptions, I kick off my shoes, and go into the kitchen. Buffy is already there drinking water from her bowl.

"Is it alright for Buffy to have a bone?" asks Taylor.

Buffy hears the word bone. Her tail pounds the floor in a frantic beat. She looks up at me wigging slightly.

"Sure," I grin as I tell Buffy "Okay" so she can pounce on the bone.

After eating the delicious fruit salad and drinking my coffee, I ask Taylor if she has any suggestions for keeping me safe from the two who obviously murdered Mr. and Mrs. McDonald.

Taylor looks thoughtful for a second, then shyly smiles. "Actually, I have been giving that some thought. As you know, I am magical. If you don't care for my idea, I understand. I can't think of anything better."

"Don't keep me in suspense. I can't think of anything decent."

"It will involve you and Buffy sort of camping out in the woods until the law catches those two and you are no longer in danger."

"But Taylor, I'm not wealthy. I need my computer to type and send my transcriptions. I can't do that in the woods."

"Jane, Darling, I know it's not ideal. I think we can work those details out. We have to keep your house safe, too. This is a little crazy, but I can make it appear your house has burned down. People will think they are seeing a burned down mess, but it will actually be invisible."

"That's all fine and dandy, but what about my job?" I press my forehead on the table covering my head with my hands.

Taylor flies over to touch my cheek. "Jane, don't despair. I believe we can arrange for electricity and an unlisted telephone, so you can continue your typing service. We are going to need official help. Why don't you call Jerry now to tell him you and Buffy are fine, but the house is a total loss. Tell him you'll be in to see him in the morning." She starts to giggle. The sound of a car stopping in front of the house stops her.

The sound freezes my insides.

Taylor whizzes out to the living room and back. "Grab your cell phone and Buffy so she doesn't bark. Those men are back. I have the house protected. We are safe. They can't get in. Let's be quiet so they think we're not here and go away. Any chance you can get a photo of them without them seeing you?"

Grabbing my phone and Buffy, we duck down behind the couch and the window in the living room. I signal Buffy to lie down. I slide my phone up over the window sill. Seeing one of the men on the display, I take a picture.

Thud! The kitchen door rattles. "Ow! I think I broke my foot. What's this door made of?"

Wham! A rock hits the window over my head. I lie down next to Buffy. She is shaking harder than I am.

"That rock flew back at me! What's this window made of?"

Wham! This time the sound is from the kitchen. "You'd think I threw a boomerang instead of a rock. It almost hit me!

"We can't get in."

"We'll get some tools and come back. Come on, Doug."

"Ow! I can't walk on this foot. Help me back to the car."

When I hear the car motor, I peek out the window. Taylor flies down to stand on the window sill. She sighs with relief, "I'm so glad the rock didn't hit him. Our *Fairy Code* requires we do no harm. Technically he threw the rock, so it would have been his own fault. But I made the window safe, so I would have had some responsibility."

"I don't understand your 'do no harm' code," I say. "If someone was trying to harm me or someone I loved, I would feel no remorse in hurting them. Can't you even protect yourself?"

"No," Taylor answers. "We can use our magic to try to defend as long as it doesn't do harm to another."

Feeling indignant I say, "If someone was trying to hurt you, I would happily hurt them instead of standing by allowing you to be injured."

"Sorry I can't do the same. Like I said, I can use magic to defend."

"Fine," I snap. "I did get several photos. If they can be identified, we might not have to do the camping thing. Let's hold off with the house fire. I'll call Jerry to tell him the men were back and I got photos. He'll want me to go into the office. I'll tell him I'm leaving Buffy with a friend and I'll be staying at her place."

Leaving Buffy at home with Taylor, I back my Subaru Forester out of the old barn. Taylor had also made sure the barn was safe, so I didn't have to worry anyone had tampered with my car.

Deputy Miller and Sheriff Baxter are waiting for me at the Sheriff's Office. I blush as I return Jerry's big smile.

"What's the address of this friend you're staying with?" asks Jerry. "I'll have extra patrols go by."

"We'll be fine."

"We need the address so we can keep an eye on you."

"There is no friend. My barn has electricity and running water, so Buffy and I will stay in it for now."

"You said those men were back," says Deputy Miller. "They could find you in the barn. It's right by the house."

"It's a hundred feet away. We'll be fine."

Jerry frowns. "You said you have pictures of the men."

"One of them; I used my phone then put them on this thumb drive."

Deputy Miller takes the drive and opens the pictures on his computer. "I know this one. It's Sam Baker."

"The other one must be Doug Rafferty," says Jerry. "They work together."

"I just remembered," I interrupt. "I heard this man call the other one Doug."

Jerry gives me another big smile. I feel my face warm. "Great!" he says. "Now we can bring them in. It isn't proof about the murder, but we can hold them for breaking and entering."

"John, put out an all-points bulletin on those two. Jane, after you write out and sign a statement about this last incident, I'll follow you home. As soon as we have those two in custody, I'll call for you to come back in and identify them for the breaking and entering charges."

I wonder what the neighbors think when I drive home followed by a police car. Jerry waves as he turns around in the drive and heads back toward town. I go into the house to talk to Taylor.

My fairy friend has typed out the medical transcriptions sent to me over the noon hour. I send them off and join Taylor in the kitchen for an afternoon snack. Jerry calls asking me to come in and identify the two men now in custody at the Sheriff's Office.

I drive back into town to the Sheriff's Office. The two men are definitely the two who came to my house. I sign a statement to that effect.

"Unless one or both get released on bail," Jerry tells me, "you should be safe. I'll call you immediately if that happens and send patrols by your house to make sure you're safe."

"Thanks, Jerry." I drive home again to find Taylor sitting on Buffy's back as she lopes around the yard.

"Jane," calls Taylor flying over to hover in front of me. "Were those the men?"

"It was. They are in jail. Jerry says we should be safe for now."

"Darling, with your permission, I'm going to stick around until you are really safe."

I sigh happily. "This may be over, but I truly appreciate you're staying. I'm enjoying being with you."

We wander into the house and settle down in the living room. We chat about plans for the rest of the afternoon. The phone rings.

"Hello."

"Jane," whispers Deputy Miller, "I can't talk or explain much now. You are in danger. Jerry sent me out of the room while he interviewed Sam Baker and Doug Rafferty. I went to another room and watched hearing them shouting at each other, blaming each other for everything going wrong. They called the Sheriff 'Boss.' Uh, I love you too, darling. I should be home in time for dinner. Miss you 'til then."

I stare at my phone and then look up toward Taylor. "Jerry seems so nice. I can't believe he's behind this?"

"That deputy sounded sincere. I'm putting the protections back up."

"I can't think what to do, Taylor. I trusted the sheriff. Let's take Buffy for a run. It will give us time to think.

"Absolutely. Let's park your car out someplace obvious to make everyone think we're someplace we aren't."

"Great idea. How about the mini-mall?"

The three of us ride down to the mini-mall. After parking the car in the huge parking lot and locking it up, we walk off to the edge of the lot. We step onto the rug and vanish from sight, flying off to the woods for our run.

Buffy seems to be having a great time. I run in silence trying to think what to do. Finally I slow down letting my heart rate and breathing relax. I haven't had any ideas to share with Taylor. She has none to share with me. My phone rings.

"Hi Jane, it's Jerry. Are you alright? I went out by your house and you weren't there. Your car wasn't there. I saw it at the mall, but couldn't find you. Where are you?"

"Hello, hello?" I shout into the phone. "Is that you Jerry? You're breaking up. I'm only hearing a few words. If you can hear me, I'm with a friend. I'll be back home in a couple of hours. Can you hear me? Hello." Turning to Taylor before disconnecting the phone I said, "I think that was the sheriff, but it was such a bad connection I couldn't tell for sure." I hang up the phone.

Taylor smiles. "Brilliant. Absolutely brilliant. Now what?"

I just shake my head. "I'm almost afraid to go back to my car. Someone may be watching it. Maybe we should just go home, and pretend not to be there."

"That's as good as anything I can think of right now. You and Buffy hop on the rug."

After our evening meal, my phone rings. I answer, knowing it will be Jerry.

"Hi, Jane. Are you home now? Your car is still at the mall. Baker and Rafferty admitted breaking into your house. Nothing was taken. They denied having anything to do with the McDonalds' deaths. I said I would let you know if those two made bail. They did."

"What about me?"

"I planned to assign Deputy Miller to keep an eye out at your house. He was injured in a hit and run."

"Oh, no! How is he?"

"Still unconscious. He might die. I can't spare another deputy. I will double the patrols going by."

"Thanks. Maybe I will take off with a friend for some shopping in Kansas City for a few days. I can use the break. Maybe you can straighten this out before I get back."

"I'll try. I wish you'd stay around here. I'd like to talk to you again. Maybe you can remember some detail to help me. Besides, I enjoy your company. We'll talk when you get back."

"I'm so sorry about Deputy Miller. I'll talk to you when we get back in a couple of days. Bye for now." I end the call.

"Oh Taylor, this is bad, bad, very bad. Now I don't even have my car here at home. All I want to do is drive and keep driving as far away as I can. I think Jerry is probably planning on having Doug or Sam kill me." I start crying.

Taylor says nothing. She keeps patting my hand.

I go to bed confident Taylor has the house protected. I finally drop off to sleep only to be jarred awake when my phone starts ringing. I grope for and turn on the light. It's two a.m.

"Hello.""Jane, Deputy Miller here.""But Jerry said you're in the hospital!"

"I am. I wasn't hurt too badly. Jerry was the driver who hit me."

"Can't you arrest him?"

"I could, but he's only a piece of this. I want the whole gang. I contacted the FBI. We need to talk to you. Jerry's looking for you. You have to be careful. Can you rent a car and come to St. Louis?"

"St. Louis?"

The FBI brought me here along with my wife for safety reasons. I'm in Barnes-Jewish West County Hospital. Can you get here? They'll come and get you, if you prefer."

"I'll make arrangements to get there."

"The phone number is new. Don't call the old one. Jerry may have it tapped."

"I'll make arrangements to get there."

"Great. Call me at this number when you get here. Bye."

"Bye."

"I came to your room as soon as I heard the phone ring," said Taylor. "I heard all of it. Pack some clothes. Put on something warm and a jacket. Bring a supply of Buffy's food. I'll provide everything else. I'll make sure the house and barn are protected. Let's get out of here as soon as possible."

I'm glad I dressed warmly for the chilly trip on the flying carpet. We arrive in St. Louis in less than the two hours it would have taken driving. I check into a motel that allows pets.

Taylor arranges breakfast for us while I call Deputy Miller.

"I'm in a motel here in St. Louis," I tell the deputy.

"You must've broken a few speed limits to get here this fast."

"I'm admitting nothing. I want to eat some breakfast. Then what do I do?"

"Come to the hospital. I'll let the FBI know you're coming."

The Ford Escort I rented by phone arrives. I head for the hospital, leaving Taylor and Buffy at the motel.

A guard stands at the door of Deputy Miller's room. He asks to see my ID before I can go in. The deputy is the only patient in the room. His arm is in a cast. Bandages are wrapped around his head.

"I'm glad you're recovering so well, Deputy Miller. Jerry said you might not survive."

"Call me John. He hoped I wouldn't. The head wound needed stitches, but is healing. The cast is a nuisance. Sit down. I'll fill you in with the little I know."

"Didn't you say your wife was here?"

"She has a room at the Holiday Inn down the road. She came by this morning then went back to shower and change clothes. She'll be back soon."

"What's going on?"

"I don't know what Jerry's doing, but the FBI had been watching him. They won't tell me much. After I called you, I checked on your file. There was no file. There was no record of your statements, the recording, the identification, nothing. I asked Jerry about it. He said he had the file. I asked to see it. He couldn't find it, told me he would send it over later."

"My shift ended. Jerry ran over me in the police lot. I didn't recognize the car and didn't see a license on it. When I woke up in the hospital, I called the FBI. They came quickly and asked a lot of questions about Jerry I couldn't answer. They called my wife and transferred me here. Then I called you."

The door opens. Two men wearing suits and ties enter flashing their ID's. "Deputy Miller, there's been a leak. We have to get you out of here now." One of the men pulls clothes out of a closet and tosses them to John.

"What about my wife?" John asks as he struggles into his clothes. The two men ignore his struggles so I try to help.

"We'll get her moved after you are situated. You are Ms. Jane Unger?"

"Yes."

"We need to talk with you. You can come with us now."

"I have a rented car. I can follow you."

"Give me the keys. We'll use it to move Mrs. Miller. Let's go."

The men rush us down the hall, one in front of us, one behind us. They punch the elevator button for the lowest floor. Once the elevator stops, we form the same group and rush to a side entrance to the hospital where a large, black sedan is waiting. I get in the back seat. John follows. One of the men sits by John next to the window. The other man gets in as the driver and starts the car, pulling out away from the curb toward the parking lot exit.

John sits quietly with a frown on his face for a minute. "May I see your ID again?" he asks the man beside him.

"Certainly." The man pulls out a revolver and points it at John.

With my heart thudding I blurt out, "You're not FBI! Who are you? Where are you taking us?" I wish Taylor were here, but what could she do? She can cause no harm to anyone.

The driver's smirking face shows in the rear view mirror as his laugh gets our attention. "Sammy Baker is my baby brother. We had a good thing going until you came along. He's rather upset with you. We'll be meeting up with him and the boss in about twenty minutes."

A car horn blares. The driver jerks the wheel to get the car back in the correct lane. I bump into John. He lands on the man with the gun and grabs for it with his good hand.

The man yanks the gun almost out of John's grasp. I lean over to help. He knocks my hand aside giving John a chance to get a better grip.

The man yanks the gun back again. This time it goes off.

The driver screams, jerking the wheel to the right; hitting a pickup truck in the next lane. He groans and slumps down over the steering wheel. His foot is still on the accelerator so the car continues on into the next lane causing brakes to squeal. I launch myself half over the seat and turn off the ignition. I grab the keys to my rented car out of the driver's pocket as the car rolls to a stop.

John has possession of the gun now. He turns it toward the man beside him. The door opens and the man falls to the ground rolling free of the car and scrambling to his feet.

The truck driver is coming toward us. "Stop that man!" I scream. "He's a kidnapper!"

John has gotten out of the sedan. Two men have grabbed our kidnapper. John starts over to where they are standing.

"He's got a gun!" someone screams. People start to scatter, opening their cell phones as they run.

"I'm a deputy," yells John. "Tell the police to call an ambulance and the FBI at Barnes-Jewish West Hospital. That's where we were kidnapped from."

"Look at my ID," yells the man trying to shrug free from the two holding him. "I'm FBI. They shot my partner. Now they want to shoot me."

Sirens sound in the distance. Three FBI agents, several police cars, plus an ambulance arrive at almost the same time.

The police start sorting out the traffic jam leaving us to the FBI. The agents show us their ID's. John looks them over carefully.

"I'm Keith Nolan," says one of the agents. "Mrs. Miller called us very upset, causing quite a commotion, when she got to the hospital and you were missing. The guard was found bound and gagged in the next room which had no patients in it."

"We're glad to see you," said John.

One of the other agents comes back from arresting one man and sending him off with police officers. The driver was put in the ambulance and was on his way to the hospital. He was gunshot and unconscious, but would probably recover.

"Everything taken care of?" asked Agent Nolan.

"What about Jerry, uh, Sheriff Baxter?" I ask. "The driver said we were going to meet him about now, actually."

"Other agents were following him. I imagine they are under arrest now. Let's go someplace where we can talk."

John and I are driven back to Barnes-Jewish West Hospital. Mrs. Miller is elated to see

John. He gets back in bed. The agents start asking questions.

Feeling exhausted from everything plus the gazillion questions, I beg to leave.

"I can't think of anything else," says Agent Nolan. "Do you need a ride back to your motel?"

"I have my keys for the rental car."

"Please stay in St. Louis for another day. We want to be sure the entire gang is in custody before you go home. Enjoy St. Louis. We'll be in touch."

The FBI gives me the all clear the next evening. The following morning Buffy, Taylor, and I return the rental car. We step onto the flying carpet and are home in time for lunch. After eating, I collapse on the couch inviting Buffy to sit beside me.

"What an awful few days," I sigh petting Buffy. "I hope this is finally over. I'm so behind on my typing."

Taylor helps me get caught up with the medical transcriptions. The phone rings as I send off the last one.

"Hello, John," I say.

"Hello, Jane. The FBI just let me know the gang is all in jail except for the driver. He's still in the hospital under guard. Sam Baker and Doug Rafferty are talking. They told the agents they killed the McDonalds on orders from Jerry. It seems there was a lucrative smuggling ring, but the couple had decided to quit. They knew too much."

"Smuggling sounds so like pirates or Prohibition."

"It's common today, too. The FBI didn't say what the gang was smuggling. I guess we have to wait for the trials to find out."

"So it's over."

"We'll have to testify unless all of them plead guilty. But we can get back to normal until then. You're home already."

"Yes."

"My wife and I will return tomorrow. Thanks for all your help."

I end the call and turn to Taylor. "You heard? It's finally over."

"Then I'm not needed here anymore. I can get back to my family."

"You have a family?" I sound shocked because I am.

"Of course I do. My husband and teenaged son are helping another family right now, they should be finished soon. Helping others is our calling. It gives us much joy. However, I admit I'm looking forward to being with them again."

"Wow! I didn't think you were much older than a teenager yourself."

"Thank you, my dear," is her sweet reply. "I'm just over seven hundred years old."

Survival

"Jean!" Jack shouted at me as he came up from the basement.

Speaking softly with obvious disdain I said, "Being your wife does not give you the right to yell at me."

Still panting from running up the stairs, Jack continued as though I hadn't spoken. "It's happened. I just heard it on the television. Hell is breaking loose all over the country. Move it! We must hurry. I'll load the chickens onto the trailer I have hooked up to the four-wheeler. You put the guns and ammo from the safe by the basement door for me to load."

"Slow down, Jack," I broke into his over-excited commands. "What do you mean 'Hell is breaking loose all over the country?' Last week the banks all closed down. What now?"

"You know we've prepared for this very thing. The whole country is going to hell in a handbasket," he yelled. "Now hurry!"

I hurried. After finishing with the gun safe, I ran back upstairs. I could hear Jack starting to haul out the things I'd put by the basement door. I unplugged everything electric. In a cooler, I put ice and food from the refrigerator. Not knowing how long we'd be gone, I then propped the door open with a chair to keep it from getting moldy.

I put my purse, extra coats, extra socks, and our boots into plastic crates by the front door along with our pictures, pills and first aid stuff, paper, pens and pencils, scissors, camera and extra batteries, and important papers like house and car titles. To that, I added our back-up files for the computers, our cameras, telephone numbers, battery-powered cell phone charger, medicines, tooth brushes, and other personal items. In another crate I loaded chips, canned goods, potatoes, onions, etc.

Jack finished carrying out the items by the front door and then disconnected our large gas propane tank.

Without speaking any other words to each

other we'd finished everything in thirty minutes and were ready to go except for the freezer in the basement. "We have time," was all Jack said.

I was scared and knew Jack was too. Yet, down we went and completely unloaded the freezer into baskets. We propped that door open also and hauled the baskets outside, putting one into the trailer for us and throwing the rest out in the yard for any critters that came along.

Shaking slightly, I jumped on the all-terrain vehicle to drive.

Jack got on behind, hugging me tightly and we took off. Jack patted my shoulder saying, "Love you."

"Love you more!" was my response and there was no more talking. I couldn't wait to ask Jack what else was happening.

I drove straight into the cave, which was in the middle of our 640 acre farm. Looking at my watch, I noticed the drive had only taken us eighteen minutes. After unhooking the trailer, Jack backed up the ATV into a dead-end area of the cave. Now there was no hurry, we'd probably be here for some time.

Jack collapsed into one of the folding chairs at the card table, looking exhausted.

"Oh, Jack, I'm so glad we kept this cave a secret and so glad you insisted we stock it for an emergency. Now, tell me what you heard on the TV."

"It's really bad," he began, holding his head with his hands. "As you know it started last week when all the banks in the whole country failed, sending the employees home and locking the doors. Riots broke out all over the United States. Now, almost every store and every filling station has closed. Nothing can be bought and paper money will probably be worthless anyway. Neighbors are robbing and killing neighbors for food and there are coke-bottle bombs going off everywhere. Ambulances are not running and even hospitals are locked up. A few doctors and nurses are staying to help the critically ill."

He took a deep breath and continued, "The police have issued a warning against terrible violence to come. There will be little or no police or fire protection according to the newscaster. He suggested people should flee the city, especially if they have campers or friends in the country. He also suggested that country people should form large groups living in one area in campers, trailers, and tents so they can protect each other from outsiders who will kill for food. The announcer stated that predictions are for millions of people dying from starvation and murder before order can be restored."

I couldn't stop the tears as Jack told me about the things he'd heard. It was worse than I could imagine. "What will happen to our kids?" I moaned. "I tried to telephone and email them before we left, but the lines must have been down. How will Jodie and seventeen-year-old Joshua survive in St. Louis? It's probably just as bad on the other side of the state where our son lives. What will Jack Jr., Brenda, and their kids do?"

Jack took me in his arms, "I know. I know." After a long pause, he whispered, "Let's pray." And we did.

***

Two months passed with little or no information from the outside world.

Occasionally a radio station would come through, but most of them no longer existed. Water was not a problem for us, but food was a challenge as we'd used up most of the supplies we had stored in the cave or brought with us. Our free roaming chickens were still giving us a few eggs.

Even though we were somewhat knowledgeable on wild plants, the small amount of food we managed to locate in the woods and fields around us soon wouldn't be enough. Fall was ending and the sweet tasting paw paws were now gone. But a few persimmons had started to ripen and we found Jerusalem artichokes, crab apples, and black walnuts.

Not using our rifles or pistols for fear of drawing unwanted visitors to our total isolation, it was a joy to see Jack occasionally coming back to the cave with a rabbit or squirrel he'd gotten with his compound bow.

We were equally thankful when, using his fishing gear, he supplied us with a few fish, frogs, or crawfish. We weren't starving; we were just bored. We had brought cards, several board games, and books to read. We slept a lot. But there wasn't much we could do without giving away our quiet, safe place of lodging.

One day while Jack went squirrel hunting with his bow I went in search of some more Jerusalem artichokes, which I could fry or boil like potatoes. As I walked, I was silently praying to God, as I often did, asking him for help for us and our kids.

Suddenly I heard limbs snapping and leaves crunching. I froze. The noisy sound of broken limbs was getting closer and closer. Breaking out in a fearful sweat, I dove into some bushes and crouched down. Then a sleek, black horse with a beautiful flowing mane came to a stop right where I was hiding and turned its head toward me. I stared into its luminescent golden eyes. This was so exciting; a horse standing very close to me.

The rider wasn't in sight, but her sweet feminine voice sounded loud and clear to me, "Fear not. I bring you important news."

My head twisted back and forth, trying to see the rider. The horse just stood there and I noticed there was no saddle or bridle. The horse could either smell me or could see me hunkered down in the brush, as its eyes seemed to stare right at me. Feeling a sense of peace, I decided to step out toward the horse. It didn't move.

"May I pet your horse" I asked, suddenly feeling quite brave.

"I'd like that," came her strange reply.

Reaching up, I stroked the horse's neck and head. "Wow! So soft and beautiful. Where are you? Come out by your horse so I can see you."

"I'm right here," came a laughing reply. "Your hand feels good stroking my head and neck."

Jerking my hand away as I stepped back, I fell on my bottom. "But… horses don't talk. I'm not sleeping, so I can't be dreaming. Oh, no, I'm losing my mind — no, I've lost it completely. It must be Alzheimer's or dementia because either I'm sitting on the ground talking to myself or talking to a horse."

"If you're finished jabbering, please get up and let's go back to your cave and wait for Jack. Then I'll explain everything. Do you want to ride or walk?"

"I'll walk," I replied, trying to make myself sound miffed when confused was more accurate. Since I had just finished asking God for help, did He send me a talking horse?

Jack arrived at the same time as the horse and me. "Jean!" he shouted, "Where'd you get the horse?"

"Ask the horse yourself," was my snotty comeback.

"Why the bad mood?" He sounded hurt.

"I'm sorry, honey. I didn't mean to snap at you," I said, kissing his cheek apologizing more quickly than normal for me.

"Okay," he grinned. "Horse, where did Jean find you?"

"She didn't find me. I found her."

Then I smiled as Jack stood there with his mouth open, saying nothing. Actually, I felt happy and swung around in a circle, grinning from ear to ear. Jack heard the horse talk too, so I wasn't that senile.

"For your information, my name is not Horse. My name is Onyx."

"A very pretty name for a pretty black horse," Jack said, quickly recovering and just stood there looking at the horse.

"Let's begin," spoke Onyx. "Would you two like to sit down? I have some very important news for you."

Jack dragged our two chairs near the cave entrance. We sat down and he put his arm over my shoulder. Smiling up at Onyx, trying to keep a grin off his face, he asked, "Good news or bad news?"

"You decide," was all Onyx said. After a pause, she began, "There is no indication that the banks are planning to re-open at this time. You may not be aware, but months ago, the president declared the entire United States to be in a state of national emergency. He asked the governors of each state to call out the National Guard. At the same time, volunteers from the Army were sent to certain areas to guard post offices, hospitals, manufacturing facilities, transport vehicles, electric power stations, certain stores, and filling stations that have agreed to re-open. The Red Cross, FEMA, and other organizations will be guarded and stocked with food and clothing to be given out in a limited amount to anyone who can verify their names and addresses. Special working computers will be used to stop people from getting more than their share.

"Great!" Jack and I jumped up and yelled at the same time. I gave Onyx a hug and thanked her for bringing us the news. "This gives us hope," I said. My eyes filled with tears.

"There's more," Onyx whispered.

"There's more," I smiled at Jack.

Taking my hand and looking into the golden eyes of Onyx, Jack grinned, "Tell us."

"Your daughter and grandson are at your house here on the farm, but they have no food or water. Your ATV would leave fresh tracks that someone might discover. If you write a note asking them to trust me, I would be happy to take it to them and bring them here to you."

"Absolutely!" Jack's voice sounded as though he were about to cry.

"Yes, please," was my response, praying we could trust the horse with our precious loved ones. I grabbed a pencil and paper and began writing.

While Onyx was gone, I asked Jack how he so rapidly accepted and trusted the talking horse. He smiled almost shyly before saying "God has taken good care of us. He is always in control. So, I try to just accept whatever comes my way, even a talking horse."

After what seemed like ages, we saw Jodie and Joshua riding on Onyx's back. They were coming slowly because riding bareback wasn't something either of them had done before. Joshua jumped down, running first to me and then to Jack.

"Grandma, Grandpa, it's terrific to see you. We have had the worst three months of our lives. It was hardest on Mom. There was violence all around. We saw gangs beating people and even killing children. There was little, and sometimes no, food or water. The good news is we've lost weight, walking over one hundred miles has made us stronger in many ways."

"Joshua, move away and let me hug my Mommy and Daddy," Jodie cried with big tears in her eyes.

Hugging her between us, Jack called Joshua to us and guided them closer to our cave. "Both of you sit down on the chairs," Jack ordered as I moved quickly into the cave and back out, bringing water for them. Kissing each of them on the cheek, saying, "I'll be right back," As I hurried inside, my heart ached seeing their thin dirty bodies, rough hands, and a beard on Joshua I'd never seen before.

Bringing them a meager lunch, I sat on the ground outside the cave next to Jack, watching them gulp down the food.

"Thanks, Mommy, Daddy. Did we just eat the last of your food? I see you two have lost weight too." Jodie's voice sounded extremely worried.

"Of course not, baby girl." Her daddy smiled, taking her in his arms. "We have not gone hungry. We just don't have the chocolate and other fatty snacks we used to eat. Feeding you two will be our joy. We're so happy to see you and have you stay here with us. Are you able to tell us about how you've survived and how you managed to get here? I understand if you don't want to talk about it though."

"As Joshua has already told you, we walked," Jodie began. "Crossing bridges was the worst because desperate people blocked others from crossing, taking their shoes and clothing and anything they had, leaving them in bad shape, sometimes even killing them. We hid and watched before crossing a bridge. Twice we had to cross rivers by swimming and continuing on in wet clothes." Jodie stopped and took a breath.

"I killed a man," came Joshua's voice in a whisper as he hung his head.

Gasping, I gave him a hug. "Oh, baby, I'm sorry you had to do that."

"Me, too," was his reply. "A guy with a knife jumped out from behind a tree, grabbing Mom and telling her to give him her shoes and clothes. I didn't think. It was just a reaction when I saw his hands on Mom. I'll tell you about it another time."

Jodie spoke up, "He wasn't the first person we saw die; he was just the first death we caused." She paused a moment, looking me in the eyes. "But," she continued, "he wasn't the last. I killed someone too."

"She saved my life," Josh defended her. "Some man twice my size was kicking and punching me."

Jodie interrupted, "Save that for another time, too. Even though it made me sick, I'm not sorry. He was really hurting my baby, I just did what I had to do."

Standing up, Jack suggested they both looked as though they needed a nap and he received no argument. He grabbed his bow and fishing pole, gave me a kiss, and waved goodbye as I took my darlings inside. I made them pallets with our extra blankets and went outside by Onyx. "Thank you, Onyx, for bringing them to us. I need to search for some food items."

Onyx knelt down saying, "Grab my mane and pull yourself on. I'll help."

Climbing on her back, Onyx slowly took me further into the woods than I'd been in a long time. We were no longer on our property, but on the five thousand acres of a designated wildlife preserve where no vehicles or horses had been allowed for the last fifty years. Onyx finally stopped, telling me to scrape some weird-looking fungus from the side of a tree.

I made a face and asked, "Are we supposed to eat that?"

After the look she gave me I slipped off her back, glad for the small trowel and bag I remembered to bring and began scraping.

Walking back to Onyx, I held up the bag to show her and she grinned at me. I must have looked shocked because I'd never seen a horse grin like that.

She just shook her beautiful mane saying, "Follow me."

When she stopped we were standing in a small field containing what looked a little like carrots and onions. "Dig some of this up and make sure you get the roots."

"What is it?" My voice spoke before my head had time to think. I got that look again before immediately dropping down, filling the bag. Onyx told me the fungus and roots could be fried, boiled, or added to soup. Onyx knelt down again, telling me to get on. Before long, we were back at the cave.

Jodie and Joshua were still sleeping. I smiled, thanking God for bringing our daughter and grandson safely to us, asking Him once again to take care of our son and his family. We couldn't help worrying about them. I cleaned the items I had harvested and started boiling the stuff for soup.

Relaxing at the cave entrance, I realized that Onyx was gone again. Then I saw her trotting toward me with Jack riding on her back.

"Ain't this great," Jack laughed, sliding off of Onyx. "I was so tired; just couldn't believe it when she came to give me a ride home, but I sure am grateful. Thanks again, Onyx."

Jack held up two skinned rabbits and two frogs. "God is so wonderful. We'll eat good tonight."

***

We enjoyed Jodie and Joshua's company. They helped us find and prepare the food and wash the clothes in the river. Two more months passed without any remarkable events to disturb our daily routines. I was still concerned about our son and his family but prayed every day for their safety. Yet, I found myself thoroughly content, enjoying the peaceful existence with Jack, Jodie, and Joshua in our cave.

What a surprise when, after breakfast one cold morning, a beautiful young woman with golden eyes and long black hair appeared at the entrance to our cave.

"Good morning, everyone," the woman

said as though she knew us and, of course, she did.

She explained that she was Onyx and, as a pooka, she had changed from horse into human form. We just stared at her in disbelief at first, but then her transformation was no harder to accept than a talking horse. Jodie let out a small giggle.

Onyx smiled and began explaining to the four of us a little about pookas, which mostly made no sense when such creatures had been just mythological before today. "Today is November Day," she announced.

"November 1st?" I questioned.

"Yes," she began. "November Day is when we pookas give more important advice and make predictions. So, I've changed to human form so you can know more about me. After we talk, you may want to try listening to your radio. Once more, there are a couple of stations broadcasting. The Army and National Guard are doing a wonderful job of trying to put the country back in order. They have arranged for several manufacturing companies to restart as well as reopening and guarding filling stations."

While Onyx talked to us, Joshua looked dazed. One look at him and I knew eighteen year old Joshua was in love. I smiled and leaned close to Jack, whispering, "How'd you like to have a pooka for a granddaughter-in-law?" Jack's look told me I had obviously lost my mind.

"My first bit of advice is for you to return to your farm," continued Onyx. "It's in a bit of mess, as several lost and hungry people stayed there for a while and have burned most of the furniture for heat. It is, however, fairly safe to live there now, except gas and electricity will be a challenge. If you have any gasoline left or can somehow purchase some, your generator can be used. There will be more service stations soon. With Federal help, more and more manufacturing and distributing facilities will soon be up and running, such as beer, food, and clothing. Banks are still closed and paper money is not being accepted yet, but silver and gold coins can be used. Some hospitals are open for emergency situations only. There are millions of homeless people. There is much healing and rebuilding to do, but things are not as desperate as before. It is still a dangerous country, but with time, it will get better."

While Onyx talked, I began to feel uncomfortable. What she was telling us was good news. However, I was happy with our cave life and felt fearful about going back home, knowing there were still lots of dangerous people around. How badly was our home torn up? Was it even livable for the four of us? But Onyx was still talking.

"I was sent to help you and your family. My job is finished."

"Wow!" I whispered to Jack. "Do you think God really sent that magical creature to us?"

His eyes lit up with a smile, planting a quick kiss on my lips. "That smart-alecky horse often reminded me of you. And yes, it is more than possible that she came from God, just like you did for me." He held my hand tightly in his.

"I'm leaving now," Onyx continued, "knowing you will help many people. I will miss you. Keep me in your memories." Onyx turned and started walking away.

"No!" yelled Josh, running and grabbing her arm. "We need to talk."

I just smiled as they walked off, holding hands.

The Horse and Dog

"Mommy," Shelly screamed. "Mommy, come quick."

I ran. Twelve-year old Shelly was in the front yard, sitting in her wheelchair smiling at me.

"Shelly, shame on you! I thought you were hurt. How many times have I told you not to yell for me unless it is absolutely necessary?"

"Sorry, I didn't mean to worry you, but look in the driveway."

Looking up the driveway I gasped a soft, "Oh." There, looking straight at us, was a beautiful black German shepherd and an even more beautiful black horse.

The driveway to our Missouri farm was about a half mile off the county road and I hadn't heard any vehicles approaching our house.

"They must be lost," Shelly whispered as though she didn't want to scare them; after she had just screamed bloody murder. "Can we keep them until we know where they belong? Please, Mommy, please."

"Probably not, Baby. If I approach them, they'll surely run away."

"At least try," Shelly begged. "Just pick up the rope hanging on the porch and try. Please. Pretty please."

I found it hard to refuse Shelly anything, even though it was a drunk driver who rear ended my car, pushing it down a ravine.

Although she'd had her seatbelt on, I felt some responsibility for the accident. Shelly received a spinal injury, which may or may not heal. At least she wasn't in pain, but she was numb from the waist down.

Taking the rope with me I walked toward the horse, fully expecting it to take off running. It didn't have a halter on and just stood there as I looped the rope around its neck. I petted it and looked at the big black dog, wondering if he would take exception to me putting a rope around the neck of his friend. I stared at him for a second because it looked as though he was smiling at me.

"Okay, Shelly, let's hope she doesn't jerk the rope out of my hands and run off with it around her neck. I'll try to walk her to the barn and then come back for you."

The horse didn't offer any resistance. She walked beside me as we went to the barn.

Our barn was empty as we had no animals. I put her in one of the horse stalls, closing the lower half of the door and removing the rope from her neck. As I left the barn, I saw that Shelly had wheeled her chair up to the open barn door, with the dog staying at her side. I felt slightly fearful, thinking to myself how weird these animals were acting. Perhaps they were sick or really hungry, although they looked well cared for.

Shelly rolled her chair up to the stall door. The horse leaned her head down for Shelly to pet, while the dog sat by the wheel chair.

Suddenly I was very scared and started to shake. That big dog could have hurt Shelly while I walked the horse to the barn. How stupid of me to leave her unguarded.

Sitting down on a bale of hay, I called, "Come, dog. Come here to me." I wanted to get him away from Shelly.

He came. He seemed friendly and he didn't look sick. I took his head in my hands and, gathering my nerves, I opened his mouth and looked at his teeth, figuring he would growl, bite, or at least pull away.

But he just sat there, letting me hold his mouth open. This seemed stranger and stranger.

"Shelly," I spoke sharply. "We are going to the house right now with no argument."

She followed me out and I shut the barn door, leaving the dog in with the horse.

I called the sheriff's office. I was told they hadn't received any calls about a missing black horse or black dog, but they'd take my name and phone number and call if they heard from anyone. They suggested I place an ad in the "Lost and Found" section of the newspaper.

I immediately called the newspaper. Then I called the vet.

He came out to our farm right away. He offered to keep them until the owners were found, but Shelly insisted we wanted them here.

A week passed with no word from the sheriff, vet, or newspaper. I began to pray that we would get to keep them as Shelly had decided they were her best friends. She said the horse was named Abby and the dog was George.

Knowing she had become very attached to them, my heart ached for her as I still expected their owners would come for them.

***

It was quite a sight watching them out of the kitchen window. They were too far away to hear, but I could tell that Shelly was talking to them. I smiled. Shelly had been leaving the door to the horse stall open for over a month now, and the horse and dog followed her as she moved slowly in her wheelchair. She'd told me that they wouldn't run away. If they did leave, I figured it was meant to be.

Sometimes Shelly would wheel under a tree and stop while the dog lay down at her feet and the horse stayed by her, too. It just didn't seem natural for the animals to have bonded to her so quickly, but Shelly loved them and was constantly petting or talking to them.

One day I looked out to see Shelly holding on to Abby's tail while her wheelchair was moving along our long driveway behind the horse. I stared when the horse came to a stop. Shelly dropped the tail and turned her chair around. Walking around her, the horse backed up, swung its tail so Shelly could grab it, and back down the driveway they came. Shelly was laughing all the way.

Another day, the dog had a rope in his mouth while Shelly held the other end and again went for a ride up and down the driveway. Circus animals, I decided. These critters must have been trained for a circus.

A few days later, as I watched again from the kitchen window, I saw the horse and wheelchair stop in the driveway. Shelly still held the tail of the horse and the horse took a step forward, pulling her up out of the chair to a standing position. My first instinct was to rush out to keep my lovely daughter from falling on her face.

Before I could react, my mouth fell open as I saw the horse back up, letting Shelly sit back in her chair. The horse took another step forward, again pulling her into a standing position and then stepped back again for her to sit down.

Realization dawned as I watched them do it again. The horse was helping strengthen those lifeless legs. I decided not to mention to my impish daughter that I realized what she was doing because I actually approved, even though I could hardly believe my own eyes.

As time went on, no one had come to claim the animals. I now thought of them as ours.

Shelly was now taking a step or two while holding the horse's tail and then the dog would push the wheelchair forward for her to sit. I was watching a miracle unfold. I decided these were not animals after all, but angels helping to heal my child's legs. I sank to my knees and thanked God over and over.

Eventually, Shelly decided it was time to show Mom how much she had improved. She stepped out of her chair, took about ten steps, turned around and came back and sat down.

With tears in my eyes, we hugged each other. "Shelly," I confessed, "I have seen you improving with the help of the angels."

"Angels?" Shelly looked confused. "You

mean Abby and George?"

"Of course," I replied, smiling.

Shelly began to giggle, turning away from me as she wheeled her chair toward the barn.

I walked back up to the porch and sat down on the swing, as the horse and dog joined Shelly, coming back toward me. Standing up, Shelly took the final steps toward the porch. "Can't take steps or do the ramp yet," she began. "Could you buy me a cane?"

As I nodded yes, she continued. "Abby and George aren't angels. I promised I wouldn't tell you about them, but they decided it was time you knew. It's a good thing you are sitting on the swing 'cause you're not going to believe this. Okay, guys," she smiled as she turned toward the animals, "you tell her."

Looking into the eyes of the animals, I saw a bit of mirth. But I wasn't prepared when the dog said, "Hi, Mom. My name is George, and I'm a pooka." Then the horse spoke, "I'm a pooka, too, and my name is Abby."

I couldn't believe what I was hearing. Then right before my unbelieving eyes, they changed into humans who looked to be in their mid-twenties.

In total confusion, I just kept shaking my head. Not only could these animals talk, they were shapeshifters or changelings. I didn't know what a pooka was, but I was pretty sure I didn't believe in them or in changelings. They must be magicians. Yes, I'd been right about the circus.

One on each side of Shelly, they put their arms around her and hoisted her up on the porch. These creatures had just touched my daughter. I rose quickly and wrapped her in my arms feeling immediately better.

"Mom," my daughter said warmly, "let's go in and sit at the table. How about cookies and milk?"

Without waiting for answers, she walked into the kitchen, putting milk, glasses, cookies, small plates, and napkins on the table before sitting down. I was still in shock, but I felt so proud of my precious child.

"Thanks," George said, stuffing a cookie in his mouth. "I haven't had oatmeal raisin cookies in ages. These are great!"

Abby obviously agreed, smiling as she nibbled on her cookie. Wiping her mouth with a napkin, she explained, "George and I have been married for three years. We chose to come live here so we could help Shelly. We may stay a few more days or many years, but eventually we may leave to help someone else."

Staring into Abby's golden eyes, I was still shaking my head in confusion.

"What's a pooka?" I mumbled, more to myself than to her.

Abby smiled and patted my hand. "We are fairies of a sort, most humans think are just myths. Some pookas, like us, enjoy helping a human heal or deal with a difficult situation. But others are quite mischievous and prefer teasing or playing tricks on people."

George spoke up, grinning, "I enjoy a bit of teasing sometimes."

"Yes, but you're never mean about it." Abby lovingly patted his hand like she had patted mine.

"Since it is the end of October," George spoke proudly with a twinkle in his eyes, "I'll fill you in about next month. November is the month of the pooka. The first day of November is called November Day, and it is common for humans to give us gifts on that day."

"Shame on you, George," Abby slapped his arm. "Please forgive him, Mom. He really is impossible sometimes. Is it okay if we call you Mom?"

"Sure. I'd like that. But even though I've now seen you in human form, I'm still struggling with believing all this."

"You will," piped in Shelly. "Give it a day or two." She was grinning so broadly it looked as though her mouth might split.

"Well, I am feeling guilty now for having you sleep in the barn at night. There are extra bedrooms in this big old farm house. Would you care to stay in the house? When you're not being a horse, of course," I stammered.

Everyone laughed.

"Yes, please." Shelly got up and hugged them. "We'll all be family. It's always just been Mommy and me. Now you can be my brother and sister, aunt and uncle, or whatever. Please stay in the house with us."

Abby looked at George and he nodded. I was still shaking my head. What a weird family we were, Shelly and me and two pookas.

Surpise! Surprise!

With the sharp knock on the door of the farm house, came the high-pitched bark of a small dog.

Looking out the window, I saw a good-looking guy in his early twenties with a cute little mustache. In the driveway was a red Jaguar that looked brand new.

Feeling slightly nervous I opened the door, while leaving the screen door latched, "May I help you?"

A smirk on his face seemed to say his good looks were all the answer I needed.

"Well," I said in irritation.

"Yes, you certainly may," he replied with that same smirk, "if you are Joyce Kay Riley. May I come in?"

Raising my seventeen-year old voice and sounding slightly snotty, "Absolutely not and my name is Joycekay, all one word. What do you want?"

He raised his tall, slim, attractive body up very straight. "I want to come in and talk to you. Is that asking too much of you?" came his sophisticated voice.

Lowering my voice, trying to make myself sound more authoritive than my seventeen years, "Before I close the door, I'll ask you one more time, what do you want?"

He quickly reached up and pulled on the screen door and laughed as he discovered it was latched.

"Come back some time when my mother is home and next time, call before you come." I yelled loudly, feeling a bit of fear while slamming and locking the door.

All he could hear then was the barking of the dog as he began knocking loudly on the door.

Feeling safer with the door locked, I turned the music up louder on the radio and went back into the office to study. I had about a month more of my home school studies over the internet before I took my finals. I would graduate from high school a year before most of the other kids my age.

Around 2:00 p.m., the telephone rang. As usual, the answering machine picked up. *'This is the Riley residence, please leave your name, number, and a brief message after the beep, and we will return your call as soon as possible.'* BEEP.

"Hello," came a female voice. "This is Mary Unger with Owensville High School. One of our employees had an eleven o'clock appointment with you this morning, Mrs. Riley, to talk about the test Joycekay will be taking next month. He reported that your daughter refused to let him talk to you. Please call us back at the school at your earliest convenience so we can get all her home schooling results before we can give her the test. Thank you and we look forward to hearing from you."

In anger, I picked up the receiver and dialed the school. "Mary Unger, please." I spoke in my most reserved voice.

"This is Mary Unger," came her voice.

"Hello Ms. Unger, this is Etta Riley. You just called here with a message about an eleven o'clock appointment this morning. I assure you that no one made an appointment to see me this morning. I was out shopping at the time a rude young man insisted on being allowed into our home. Joycekay was home alone at the time and wisely did not let the stranger into our house. She asked him twice what he wanted. He did not reply the first time he was asked and the second time he replied that he wanted to come in. Joycekay told him to come back sometime when I was home and to call ahead. I believe she handled the situation very well, in spite of the poor behavior of your young man."

"Please call me Mary," was her sweet reply. "I apologize for the misunderstanding. Angus McDuff assured me he had an appointment."

"He did not," I shot back showing more anger than necessary. "My daughter is right here and neither of us was contacted for an appointment."

"Once again, I am very sorry. Would it be convenient for him to come by tomorrow?"

"No, it would not," I softened my voice. "Let me know when it is convenient for you and we will drop the necessary paperwork off to your office."

"That will be fine," she answered softly.

"Any time after ten a.m. tomorrow. I look forward to meeting you. Bye now."

Hanging up the phone and with a heavy sigh, I sat down. One more month. I just had to last for one more month.

***

No one at the school knew me. I felt nervous, but knew I looked like all the rest of the kids wearing jeans and a tee shirt. Arriving before the lunch hour, I roamed the hall near the office, often pausing at a locker as though to open it.

Eventually, the office door opened and a nice-looking woman in her 50's wearing a navy blue skirt and white blouse came out and headed toward the restroom. I quickly entered the office and laid the paperwork on the secretary's desk and, sighing with relief, left just as quickly. Mission accomplished.

Jumping into my old Ford truck, I quickly returned to the farm, went to the office, and began my studies again.

***

A couple of hours later, Mary Unger left a telephone message thanking Mrs. Riley for Joycekay's homeschooling information and saying she was sorry they had missed each other.

Smiling to myself after hearing the message, I decided to saddle J.F. and go for a leisurely ride. For a stallion, J.F. was always a gentleman with me.

We followed the creek that flowed through the field in back of the barn for a while and then headed up toward the apple orchard. There I dismounted, dropping the reigns over J.F.'s head, knowing he'd stay close to me.

I picked two apples from the tree, gave one to J.F., and sat down to read my history book. I tried, but couldn't concentrate.

I thought back to the telephone call from Mr. Butler, my grandmother's lawyer. Mrs. Myers, the foster mom I had been living with in St. Louis, Missouri, handed me the phone and politely went back to the kitchen to finish cooking dinner. I really liked her. She didn't show much affection to me. She was firm and insisted I help with the chores and do my homework. Yet she never raised her voice or put me down. She actually seemed to respect me and seemed to like having me in her home.

"Hello," said the male voice on the telephone. "Is this Joycekay Riley?"

"Who wants to know?" was my reply.

"My name is Richard Butler. I was the lawyer for Etta Riley's mother, Mrs. Louie Morgan, who recently passed away. After much research, we have discovered her daughter, Etta Riley died about a year ago and you are the only living relative of Louie Morgan. We need to meet in order to discuss your inheritance. My office," he continued, "is in Rolla, Missouri. Ordinarily, I would ask you to come here, but since you are a minor with no legal guardian, I am willing to come to St. Louis to meet with you."

I smiled remembering that conversation. After he told me there was money, a truck, and property involved, I smiled remembering my confusion and my distrust. My mother had never told me about a grandmother and I had asked about having any relatives several times. She never actually said there was no one. She would either ignore me or shake her head leaving me thinking we had no living relatives.

I had told the lawyer I would prefer to take a bus to Rolla if he would then transport me to the property involved. Having passed my driving test, I had already received my driver's license, and thinking about owning a truck and property felt exciting, like winning the lottery. I looked forward to meeting him, but had worried that perhaps it was some sort of scam and perhaps I would be in danger. I went though, believing I could take care of myself.

Bringing my mind back to the present, I tried once again to concentrate on my history book. No go. My thoughts just kept going back to that time in my life just three short months ago.

After the short meeting in Mr. Butler's office, he had taken me to my grandmother's farm outside of Owensville. There he had introduced me to her neighbor, Mr. Bergmann, who explained he had taken care of the property and of the stallion since my grandmother had died. I remembered my excitement. A horse. I would have this farm, a truck, and a horse.

Mr. Bergmann had insisted the stallion, J.F., was mean as a snake and for me never to try riding him. He said all he did was open the stall gate in the morning so the horse could go outside into the fenced-in lot. Then in the evening, Mr. Bergmann came back to the barn and put grain in the feed trough for him and would stand back while J.F. would go back into his stall and allow Mr. Bergmann to close the gate.

Mr. Richard Butler filed papers and became my legal guardian and arranged with the Missouri Department of Social Services for me to live with him and Sarah, his wife. I was finishing my last home schooling subjects for high school graduation over the internet.

After much begging, he agreed that now that I was seventeen and very mature for my age, he would allow me to stay at the farm alone. For a while he came out to check on me every few days. Now it was just every week or two.

It had taken J.F. less than two weeks to let me ride him, lift his feet up for grooming, and let me walk completely around him without worrying that he might kick me when I was behind him. He was gorgeous and gentle with me and I learned to love him with my whole being.

Trying without success to study my history book again, I was having a hard time keeping my eyes open.

J.F. had stopped nibbling grass and came over close to me and lay down. I fell asleep.

Waking up, the sun was gone and a light drizzle started falling on my face, J.F. and I made our way back to the farm.

I brushed him good and gave him his grain and, since I no longer closed his stall gate, I slowly made my way out of the barn. I came to a sudden stop, seeing the red Jaguar in front of the house, with Angus leaning against the hood.

"What are you doing here?" I shouted angrily at him.

"Waiting to see you?" he said with a killer grin. "Your mother isn't home; at least she isn't answering the door. My assistant said she would make the appointment to see your mother the other day and I assumed she had. I wanted to apologize."

"Fine, apology accepted. I have a lot to do, if you'll excuse me," I said sarcastically over my shoulder as I started toward the porch.

"Hold on," he snapped, rushing forward and grabbing my arm. "I had another reason for coming here. I want you to come into town and have pizza with me."

"I don't give a flying shit what you want Mr. Angus McDuff," I said in a low angry voice. "I have no intention of having pizza with you now or ever."

His face turned beet red. Before I realized what was happening, he grabbed me by the throat and started dragging me toward the barn.

"You need a lesson, little lady. I'm willing to be the guy to teach you some manners."

I was finally able to let out a blood curtailing scream.

"Mommy's not home, is she?" he said sarcastically. "Scream all you want, there's no one to hear you."

I was still struggling and had managed to scratch his arm and face, when the most beautiful man I'd ever seen appeared;

wrapping his big muscled arm around Angus
and slammed him to the ground.

"Hi cousin Joycekay," he drawled. "Do you
want me to kill him for you?"

I was still sitting on the ground where I'd
fallen, still feeling shaky. I gradually stood up.
"No, not right now. But would you please
hold him in front of you, facing me," I asked
with a gleam in my eyes. I hauled back and
kicked him in the balls.

"Now, cousin, would you please help him
to his car and assure him that if he tries that
on me or any other girl, that you are willing to
teach him some manners. I'll be in the house
washing his filth off me." I ran.

After a quick wash, I walked to the window
to see that the Jaguar was gone. I opened the
front door wondering where that gorgeous
man had gone. I walked to the barn and saw
J.F. standing peacefully in his stall. No one
was around. Walking back to the house, I tried
convincing myself that what happened was
real. But where had the mysterious man come
from and where had he gone. I knew I didn't
have any cousins. Or did I? I hadn't known
about my grandmother. I kept wondering

where he had gone?

After quickly eating a pot pie cooked in the microwave, I read a little of my history book in bed before falling asleep, dreaming of my knight in shining armor.

In the morning, after greeting J.F. and following him out into the pasture, I told him all about my experience the night before after leaving him in the barn. As always, he gave me his full attention as he listened to me, even resting his large head on my shoulder. "I love you J.F., I'll be back after I have breakfast and do a little homework."

***

One week before I was due to go to the Owensville High School for my final test, the red Jaguar showed up at my farm house. I watched him slowly walk to the front porch glancing around, especially toward the barn.

There was the shrill yipping of the dog as he knocked on the door. Cautiously opening the door while leaving the screen door latched, I said, "Angus, you have a lot of nerve. What do you want?"

"I want to sincerely apologize for my behavior when I was last here. I don't know what came over me. I know I am spoiled and used to getting what I want. I just lost it when you treated me as trash."

"I still think you are trash and want you to leave before I call 911." I lifted my arm up, showing him the phone in my hand.

"That wouldn't be in your best interest," he said giving his hips a kind of swagger. "I know that you don't have a mother or grandmother. They are both dead. At seventeen you are still under age living here on your own. If I report you to the authorities, they will come get you and you won't be able to take your high school final. So," he paused, "let me inside, play nice, and I won't report you."

Feeling quite smug, knowing Mr. Butler had given me permission to be on my own, I lowered my hand that held the cell phone and dialed 911.

Angus and I heard the phone say, "What is your emergency?"

"Angus McDuff is at my house threatening to rape me. Please help." And with a nasty smile on my face, I hung up before she could reply.

"You stupid bitch!" Angus shouted as he ran to his car. "You'll be sorry."

I quickly dialed Richard Butler in Rolla, explaining everything to him.

"I'll be there in about 40 minutes. Try to hold the sheriff off until I get there," he quietly spoke before saying goodbye.

I ran to the barn to cry into J.F.'s silky mane. But instead of J.F., my wonderful knight stood in the stall.

"Hi," he smiled as I came to a skidding stop.

I was too speechless to talk.

"I saw Angus drive up and was about to come to your rescue, then he came sailing off the porch and roared away in his 'jag. I thought we could continue our lives as we have been but I suspect we have a lot to talk about before Richard Butler and the sheriff gets here."

I nodded feeling overwhelmed.

"I'll go first," he smiled, "but first you need to sit down."

I sat on a bale of hay.

"May I sit beside you?"

I quivered, nodding again; scooting over to give him room, feeling safe but confused. I couldn't help staring at his handsome face. I felt warmth climb up my leg as his leg touched mine.

He took my hand saying, "May I?"

I nodded.

"You are not going to believe what I am about to tell you, but please wait and I'll prove it. Okay?"

I nodded, hoping I didn't have a silly grin on my face, but he was wonderful to look at.

"First of all, I am J.F. when I am a horse and John Frances Knight when I'm human. I'm a pooka and I can change from horse to human whenever I want."

My mouth fell open.

"You don't believe me, do you?" he sounded a little sad.

"I actually do believe you," I gasped as I started laughing and couldn't stop.

He dropped my hand and stood up. "Is that so funny or are you going hysterical on me?"

Getting myself under control, I muttered, "I didn't know I was a pooka." I grinned from ear to ear. "I thought I came from outer space or was just magical." And there on the bale of hay, instead of me, sat a small white fluffy dog.

"My dear Father in Heaven," was John's response as he sat down and picked me up. Then both of us discovered we didn't need speech.

In my dog form, I thought to him, "*Should I lick your hand or bite it?*"

He thought back to me, "*I sincerely hope you'll change back to human form because I'd rather not French kiss this dog.*"

Changing back into human form, I was still sitting on his lap with his arms around me. He took my head in his hands and kissed me silly.

"Joycekay, I'm glad we aren't really cousins. Even though we haven't known each other very long, one day we are going to be man and wife. I'm older than you and right now you are still jail bait. We are going to take our time to get to know each other better. Please know now and forever, that I love you. I always will."

"Johnny, I love you too." It felt natural calling him Johnny instead of J.F. "I loved you even when you were a horse; I hope that doesn't make me a sicko. I love you even more now. The sheriff will be here soon and so will Mr. Butler. He'll explain everything to the authorities. I might have to live with him and his wife until I'm eighteen, but if so, you can live here. I will be taking my final test at school next week, to get my graduation certificate." Pausing a second, I felt giddy and knew I was talking too fast.

"Johnny, I have a serious question for you. Does this mean our children will be little pookas?"

Jodie and Her Magical Dogs

"Jodie, wake up!" Sky Queen's wet tongue licked Jodie's face since the dog's words were having no effect.

"Yuck," she moaned as she rolled over.

"You were having your nightmare again."

"Okay, okay, I'm awake now. Go away." She tried sounding as pathetic as possible.

"The sun is up. Jade ate all our kibble; I'm hungry. If you don't get up soon, I'll knock over the food container so I can help myself."

"Bad dog, bad dog!" Jodie raised her voice, as she sat up rubbing her eyes. "The last time you did that, there was kibble all over the kitchen."

The white German Shepherd Dog smiled. *"Thought that would get your attention. Jade and I have already been outside. Hurry up, bathe, get dressed, and come into the kitchen so we can eat.*

105

It's going to be a busy day."

"Fine," she complained. "I'm the human. I am supposed to be the boss. It is all wrong to let dogs, even talking dogs, run my life. This is going to end. Do you hear me?" Jodie was aware Sky heard her. She saw the tail wag as she pranced out the bedroom door.

Jodie felt grumpy, even though she knew Sky Queen was right. It didn't keep her from trying to think of some way to keep her dogs from ordering her around. She decided she'd call her mom right after breakfast.

She showered quickly, and then hurried into the kitchen after pulling on a ragged pair of jeans, along with a bright blue tee-shirt.

"Hi, Jodie," both dogs said at the same time.

"Hi yourselves, you mongrel mutts," Jodie mumbled at them. Of course, they knew they weren't mongrels. Sky is a German shepherd dog, whose parents Frank and Fancy, live at Jodie's parent's house. Jade's parents, Bob and Bonnie, standard poodles, also live with her mother and father. Sky and Jade's parents can talk just as they can. Jodie's parents had allowed both Bonnie and Fancy to have three litters of puppies, after which they were spayed. One female puppy from each litter could talk, which meant Sky and Jade each had two sisters somewhere that could speak.

Since it was Saturday, Jodie fried bacon and eggs. She shared them with the dogs although normally they only received kibble to eat. Saturdays were their favorite day of the week. Jodie got about three eggs a day from her hens, which was more than she usually used, as she normally ate cereal on work days. Her parents enjoyed receiving the fresh eggs from her.

She had rinsed the dishes and put them into the dishwasher when the telephone rang. Jodie listened as the answering machine announced the call was from Becky, her secretary.

"Hi, Jodie," she began. "Sorry to bother you on Saturday, but Lieutenant Harold Nelson called, demanding to talk to you. He said it was urgent."

Jodie picked up the phone. "Hi, Becky. Thanks for the message. I have his number. I'll call him back. Have a good weekend. Bye."

Telephone calls usually bored the dogs and, as usual, they raced each other out the doggy door to go for a run in the wooded area in back of her house.

After two rings, Harold Nelson answered with a gruff "Hello."

"Hi, Harold," Jodie replied. "What is so urgent? You know I only go in to work at my computer company office Mondays, Wednesdays, and Thursdays. I especially don't work on weekends."

"Sorry gorgeous, but I don't have that luxury. The 'Cowboy' struck again last night. This time we have a witness who dialed 911 and made the report. The problem is that he is only four years old. Social Services has him, but won't let us talk to him. I need you and your dogs to work your magic, please, pretty please. We need to move fast on this before 'Cowboy' gets wind of him. He'll probably try to harm him."

"This is a low blow, Harold, using a child to make me work when you know how important my weekend time is to me."

Before Jodie could say more, Lieutenant Nelson gave her a name, address, and phone number, after which he made kissing noises at her as he hung up.

"Jerk," she shouted at the empty phone line.

She called Missouri Department of Social Services in St. Louis immediately, asking for Ann.

"Hello, Ann. I have to make this quick. As you are aware, I am current on my foster parenting training. I want you to arrange for that four year old whose mother was just killed to be placed in my care immediately. You know my dogs and I will be good for him. This is very important to me, so do whatever you need to do. I'll be at your house in an hour to get him. Love ya', bye."

Jodie went to the door and yelled, "Sky, Jade, come home now." Closing the door, she didn't wait to hear from them. She grabbed their service halters, leashes, her purse, and a car seat for the boy. She started for the car, thankful that the gas tank was full.

Both dogs were panting from their run while Jodie strapped on their harness vests, explaining to them about heading to Walmart for quick shopping. She explained to them about going to visit a traumatized little boy who needed their help.

Both dogs trotted close to her, Jade on her left as usual while Sky stayed on her right. As service dogs they were allowed in the store. Jodie purchased milk, cookies, and a superhero cape.

As Jodie drove to Ann's house, she reflected on how fortunate it was that they'd been friends since college. Ann's position at the Department of Social Services allowed Jodie to skip a lot of red tape when she needed to get things done. Before she knew it, Jodie was pulling into the driveway of Ann's ranch style house.

When Ann opened her door to them, the dogs laid down as soon as they were inside. Their training included teaching them how often children were afraid of dogs, especially big dogs like them. Laying down was much less threating to children. This allowed a child to choose whether or not to go to the dogs.

The boy was obviously scared as he sat in the middle of Ann's living room couch.

"You owe me, girlfriend," Ann whispered. "There was a lot of discussion on where to place Ronnie. I had to throw not only my own weight, but a few names like governor and mayor before they gave him to me. They have copies of your license of course and will be contacting you at your house this afternoon. Now, start doing your magic on him while I watch."

"Ronnie," I spoke to him softly. "Would you like to pet my dogs. They want to be your friends. They can talk to you. Did you know that?"

Ronnie's eyes widened slightly in obvious disbelief.

"Hello, Ronnie," Sky spoke. Ann and Jodie could also hear her.

Ronnie's head tilted slightly to one side and looked first at the dogs, then at Jodie. "How'd you do that?" he asked.

Jodie shook her head and waited.

"Hey, Ronnie," began Jade as she pointed her nose at me. *"Her name is Jodie and she didn't do that. My name is Jade. The white dog is Sky. Did any other dog ever talk to you?"*

Ronnie shook his head.

"Hey, Ronnie, buddy," Sky spoke up. *"Is it okay if I come over to the couch by you?"*

"I guess," the child replied.

Slowly, Sky walked toward the couch,

turned around as she neared it, and sat with her head pointing away from the boy.

Ronnie started reaching his hand to Sky, but pulled back.

"*Say, my friend,*" Sky spoke again. "*I do have an itch on the back of my head. Would you mind scratching it a bit?*"

Slowly, Ronnie reached his fingers toward Sky, gently scratching.

"*Ah, that is great. You are awesome. Thanks a lot.*"

Ann turned her smile at Jodie.

She shrugged and smiled back.

"*Ronnie, would you like it if I kissed your hand?*"

"Huh," was his only sound.

"*You know, I'll just turn my head around and lick your hand. That's my way of giving you a kiss.*"

Hesitating at first, Ronnie finally nodded.

Gradually, Sky turned her head toward Ronnie's hand and licked it once.

Ronnie giggled as he pulled his hand back. "Can the other dog do that too?"

"*You bet I can. I'll come right over to you,*" Jade said.

Ronnie stretched his hand toward Jade, smiling when the dog's tongue moistened it.

"When we kiss your hand," Jade said, *"you are supposed to say, thank you."*

"Oh, I didn't know," Ronnie sounded contrite. "Thank you, Jade. Thank you, Sky."

"You are welcome," both dogs spoke at once.

"Hey kid, would you like to come see our house? Maybe you could even stay and play with us for a while?"

"Sure, if you think it would be okay with my mom."

"I think your mom would like that very much," Jade said, licking his hand again.

"Thank you, Jade," Ronnie smiled. "Let's go."

"Hang on to my harness," Sky said. *"We'll walk to the car together."*

Ann gave Jodie a hug, handing her a small bag with clothes and toys. "Are we still on for lunch Tuesday? Call me," she ordered.

Jodie nodded, whispering, "Yes, but at my house instead of Tony's Restaurant. I have a child now," she smiled as she followed Ronnie and the dogs to the car.

The day was going well. Ronnie pretended

to be a superhero, rescuing the dogs until lunch time. He fell asleep on the living room rug with his head resting on Jade's belly and Sky at his feet. The social workers came early in the afternoon. They only needed to talk with Jodie for a few minutes to make sure everything was in order and were soon on their way.

After they left, Jade, Sky, Ronnie and Jodie went for a walk before it was time to fix dinner. Ronnie was starting to get a bit restless and twice asked for his mommy. The first time Jodie tried explaining to him that his mommy was in Heaven with God and couldn't come home. The second time Sky did the explaining. Ronnie seemed to accept their explanations until it was time for bath and bed. Jodie tried rocking and comforting him, but it didn't work. He ended up crying himself to sleep, holding Jade close like a large teddy bear.

In the morning, he was up early with the dogs. Catching him as he was climbing out the doggy door after Jade and Sky, Jodie persuaded him to have breakfast first.

He cheerfully ate his cereal, saying, "Good

cereal, Aunt Jodie."

She smiled, wondering where he came up with the 'Aunt Jodie' name.

"You're not my mommy. My mommy is dead." He sighed sadly. "So, will you be my Aunt Jodie?"

"I will like being your Aunt Jodie very much. Does that mean you'll give me lots of hugs?"

"Okay," he grinned as he got up from the table to hug her.

Jodie told the dogs she was going to try to talk to Ronnie about witnessing his mother's murder, saying he would need them for comfort. "Ronnie, do you remember seeing your mother being shot?"

Looking at her with wide eyes, he nodded.

"Can you tell me what you saw?"

Jade nudged his hand for petting.

With his hand gently on Jade's head, he softly said, "A bad man blooded her with a gun."

"How?"

"The gun went 'bang' real loud. Mommy fell down and bleeded."

"Where were you?"

"Hiding behind the half wall at the top of the stairs."

"Did he see you?"

"Don't know. He ran out the back door."

"Thanks for telling me, honey. You can talk to me about it anytime, okay?"

He nodded sadly.

Later she called Lieutenant Nelson, "Nelson here."

"Hi, Harold, it's Jodie. I'm going to be Ronnie's foster mom. Wanted to update you on my conversation with him; I doubt he'll be much help, but time will tell. He was hiding behind the half wall on the second floor. It doesn't sound as though he was seen. He heard and saw her shot and saw her bleeding. I imagine he went down to her, but don't know yet. You've already told me that he dialed 911. That's all I've discovered so far. I can't push him and I advise against you trying to talk to him yet.

***

A week later, an hour after Jodie had taken Ronnie to the town's playground, he came running back to her crying. She had been watching him very closely and didn't see how she could have missed him being hurt. He had been playing with a little girl named Cindy. Maybe she'd bitten him. Cuddling him, she finally got him calmed down enough to learn he wasn't physically hurt.

"Cindy says I'm a liar," he sobbed.

"Oh baby, why does she think you're a liar?"

"I told her about Sky and Jade talking to me," he spoke, hanging his head.

"Ronnie, darling, I told you that is a special secret and no one must ever know."

"I forgot," he sniffled. "She was bragging about her stupid cat, meowing to her, like it was talking to her, so I told her my dogs speak to me in words." With pleading eyes, Ronnie looked up at her asking, "Will I have to leave your house because you're mad at me?"

"Of course not, sweetheart. I'm not mad at you. I love you. But I doubt that anyone will ever believe the dogs talk to you in words. So, if you tell anyone else, you'll probably be called a liar again."

"How 'bout she comes to our house and hears the dogs talk?"

"Sorry, Ronnie, they've been trained never to talk to people without my permission and I don't want people to know what they can do. I won't give them permission to talk. In fact, honey, if I told them they could no longer talk to you, they would obey me. If you want to continue hearing them talk to you, you must never tell anyone else. And you will have to accept that Cindy thinks you are a liar, unless you tell her you are sorry for what you said. She will probably think that means they can't really talk in words and she'll forgive you. Do you understand?"

"Yes, Aunt Jodie, I understand. Can we go home now? I don't want to tell Cindy I'm sorry, and I don't want to play with her any more. Is that okay?"

"Of course it is, my precious boy. Let's go home."

Ann showed up Tuesday at noon for lunch. Jodie explained the menu had been adjusted to suit a four-year old. The spaghetti, French bread, and salad were enjoyed with plenty of butter and jelly for the bread. Dessert consisted of blueberry muffins, again loaded with butter and jelly.

Ann and Jodie cleared the table, putting items in the dishwasher and leftover spaghetti in the refrigerator. They enjoyed sitting on the porch watching Ronnie and the dogs playing fetch and tag.

In a low voice Ann said, "I gather you didn't watch the ten o'clock news last night."

"No, why?"

"There was another murder yesterday evening, apparently by the serial killer they're calling Cowboy. In the same announcement the newsman stated that it was another blonde in her early thirties, but this time there were no children in the house unlike the last murder where a small child may have witnessed his mother being killed. Even though the name of Ronnie's mother wasn't mentioned, it's been in the papers, television, and radio broadcasts."

"Oh Ann, this is awful! Ronnie is in danger. I think we might have to go into hiding for a while."

"Where? I could get you permission to take Ronnie out of our county, but it would be difficult to get authorization to take him out of state; and what about Pleasant Computer

Company?"

"I don't know. Give me a minute to think."

"Okay."

"Ann, first of all, I need you to get authorization for me to take Ronnie out of state. We have Pleasant Computer Companies all over the United States. Sometimes, I have to travel to different places to solve a problem. I've even taken the dogs with me several times. Sometimes I work from home like I do on Tuesdays and Fridays. I can still work and do my job and keep Ronnie safe as I travel with him and the dogs to different company locations across the country."

"I don't know, Jodie, doesn't sound like a good life for Ronnie."

"Nonsense, he doesn't start kindergarten for over a year. He'll love it. Let me think. Let me think."

"Go ahead and think," said Ann with a frown.

"I've got it! My sister Denise's husband died in an automobile accident six months ago. She was a stay-at-home wife and had unsuccessfully been trying to get pregnant. Since she is financially secure, she still hasn't tried seeking employment. Denise needs something to get her out of the house. I'd bet my best pair of gloves she'd love to come with me and help take care of Ronnie and the dogs when I have to call on one of our companies. I might even buy a camper to pull behind a new truck I might also buy. That will keep us from needing motels all the time. I can certainly afford it."

"I don't know, Jodie. This couldn't all happen in a day or two. It'll take time."

"The sooner we start the sooner we can leave." Those words were barely out of Jodie's mouth, when they heard Jade barking and Sky's growls. Standing up, Ann and Jodie couldn't see what was upsetting the dogs. Ronnie was standing still, looking at something they couldn't see around the corner of the house.

Rushing down the steps, Jodie grabbed Ronnie, hugging him close and Ann went to the dogs in order to see what was causing their concern.

Ronnie started crying, "Bad man, Jodie, bad man."

Jodie rushed into the house carrying Ronnie

without waiting for her friend. Stay with Ann," she ordered the dogs.

Still holding Ronnie, Jodie grabbed the phone and dialed 911 while going to another window where she could see Ann, the dogs, and a man wearing a hoodie that partially covered his face.

"What is your emergency?" came the 911 voice.

Jodie quickly gave her name and address, explaining there was an unidentified man in her yard that she believed was trying to kidnap her child. "My dogs and my friend Ann Wilson with Missouri DSS are still out near the man. Call Lieutenant Harold Nelson with the St. Louis police department immediately for more information on my situation."

"We are sending immediate help and are calling Lieutenant Nelson. Please stay on the line."

"I will but I'm handing the phone to my four-year old to free up my other hand. I have to lock doors and windows."

Jodie felt a little guilty locking Ann out. She knew Ann was licensed to carry, but didn't know if she had her pistol on her. She always carried pepper spray in her pocket. Locking up quickly, Jodie went back where she could see Ann. She was standing about ten feet from the guy with one hand in a fist, where Jodie assumed she was holding her pepper spray.

Jodie couldn't hear what was being said, but the dogs could and they were standing one on each side of Ann. With her free hand she was pointing to the ground. If she was telling the man to get on the ground he didn't do it. He kept glancing at the dogs as if trying to decide if they'd attack him.

Police sirens could be heard a few minutes later. The man turned and ran, disappearing from sight. Ann put her pepper spray in her pocket and petted and talked to the dogs. The three of them walked to the gate, opened it and went to wait for the officers by the front door.

Explaining to the 911 lady, that the police were here, Jodie hung up and unlocked and opened the front door.

Jodie and Ann were still explaining things to the uniformed officers when Lieutenant Harold Nelson showed up about fifteen minutes later. He ran through the front door and wrapped Ronnie and Jodie in a hug. "Are you two alright?" he asked.

Nodding, Jodie started to shake. She'd been fine until Harold hugged her. She didn't cry because she didn't want to frighten Ronnie, but it was difficult for her.

Ann, Jade, Sky, and the two officers came in and everyone sat down in the living room.

Ann explained that the man seemed shifty, but didn't act aggressively toward her. "The dogs growling from time to time seemed to keep him in line. When I asked him why he opened the gate and came onto private property uninvited, he said he wanted a closer look at the poodle because he had one that looked like her but was stolen from him. I didn't believe him of course, and when I asked him to get down on the ground he laughed and refused, but still he didn't attempt to leave until we heard the sirens."

"Would you be able to recognize him?" asked the Lieutenant.

"I'm fairly certain I could," Ann said. "His hoodie covered one of his eyes, however I could see the other one and I was only about ten feet away from him."

"Jodie, how about you?"

"No Harold, I never got a good look at him. His body was turned slightly away from the window when I was looking at him."

Ronnie began squirming as I still held him on my hip. "Bad man," he whispered.

"Hi, Ronnie," Lieutenant Harold looked at him. "Have you seen that man before?"

Ronnie nodded, "He shooted my mommy with his gun and ran out the back door."

"Thanks, Ronnie. That's a big help," smiled Lieutenant Harold.

Jodie put Ronnie down. He sat on the floor next to the dogs and began petting them. "Thanks Jade and Sky. You saved me."

They didn't reply.

"Oh, I forgotted," Ronnie whispered.

"What'd you forget, Ronnie," asked the Lieutenant.

"Nutten," replied Ronnie. "Just wanted to thank Sky and Jade."

Lieutenant Harold smiled at him.

Jodie and Ann grinned at each other knowing he'd forgotten the dogs wouldn't talk while Lieutenant Harold was there.

Ann gave Harold a hug saying, "If you no longer need me, I've got to run."

"I'll walk you to your car," Harold said hugging Jodie and shaking hands with Ronnie.

As soon as Harold left, Jodie bent down to pet both dogs. "Yes, thank you girls," Jodie whispered.

"*You're welcome,*" Jade said at the same time Sky said, "*My pleasure. Truly, it was my pleasure, but biting him would have given me even more pleasure.*"

"You know that would have been wrong, Sky. Even though we are sure he was a bad person, he was not showing any aggression. If you had bitten him, you would have been the aggressor and you and I would both be in trouble."

"*I know that,*" Sky sounded in a huff. "*That's why I didn't bite him. I was only letting you know that it would have given me pleasure to do so.*"

Later that evening, Ann called Jodie.

"Hello, Ann," Jodie said, looking at the caller ID.

"Hi, girlfriend. Wanted to let you know that Harold asked me to go with him to look at mug shots. Sorry I couldn't find one of the guy at your place today. However, I did get permission for you to take Ronnie out of our county and into any US state."

"That's wonderful. I suppose finding his photo would have made it too easy, but being able to leave the state is the most important thing. I got permission to begin immediately visiting and supervising our out-of-state offices and warehouses. I'll be reporting back to our head office here in St. Louis after each visit."

"Great. What about your sister?"

"Denise is thrilled with the idea and has already started packing. I took Ronnie and the dogs to the Ford dealer today and bought a Ford 350, four-door truck, including a matching topper. They will deliver it to my house a few weeks from now when I call them. Then we drove to Wentzville and I bought a Coleman travel trailer. I won't pick it up until I have the truck, after I get back from this first trip. I'm leaving the dogs with Mom and Dad for now. Denise, Ronnie, and I are flying out in the morning to California. I'll email you our agenda."

"Wow, you accomplished a lot this afternoon."

"Sure did. I'm exhausted. Ronnie got a nap on the ride back from Wentzville. Now I've got a lot of packing to do. In the morning, after picking up Denise, we drop off Jade and Sky and head for the airport."

After the call from Ann, Jodie called Lieutenant Harold Nelson.

"Nelson," he answered.

"Hi, Harold. I have a favor to ask. Could you or one of your officers watch my house tonight. Ronnie and I and my sister are flying out on a business trip in the morning. I am concerned Cowboy may come by again."

"Sure, Babe. I'll join you in bed to make sure your safe."

"In your dreams, buster. That'd be like sleeping with a brother, which I don't have. It ain't ever gonna happen."

"Can't blame a guy for trying."

"I can and might throw a harassment charge at you."

"Aw, you don't want to do that. Then you'd have to stop calling me so much."

"Good point. Gotta' go. Love ya'. Bye."

Harold arrived just after ten with a blanket and pillow. "Hi, doll. Don't give me any argument. I'm not sitting in my car outside all night. I'll be on the couch."

"Come inside and check it out. The sheets are already on the couch, including pillow and blanket."

Laughing, Harold said, "I expected as much, just wasn't taking any chances. Night."

"Sleep tight. No, no! I mean sleep light, just in case."

No answer. He had already removed his shoes and was climbing under the blanket.

***

Ronnie cried saying goodbye to Sky and Jade and Jodie teared up. Denise said, "Suck it up, sis. We've got to get to the airport."

Jade, the tease, said, *"Bye, Jodie. Wish I could say I'll miss you, but I can't wait to play with my mom and dad. Bye, Ronnie, I'll miss you lots."* She licked his hand and he stopped crying and said, "Thank you."

"Bye, Buddy. I'm going to miss you lots too," as Sky also licked Ronnie's hand and heard

Ronnie's "thanks."

"*Don't worry about us. We love coming here to the farm and playing with our parents and the other animals. Have a nice time on your trip, okay?*"

"Okay," he whimpered.

***

"Hi, Ann, it's been a long three weeks. After dropping off Denise and picking up the dogs, Ronnie and I are home. He is in the living room now chatting with them. All three of them keep interrupting each other. Ronnie tells about the trip and Jade and Sky talk about the farm."

"Wonderful to have you back. Is it alright if I come spend the night so we can catch up?"

"I'd love that. What time will you be here?"

"I'll pick up pizza and be at your place around six. I can stay until two tomorrow afternoon."

"Good, we'll talk more later. Bye."

Calling Lieutenant Harold, Jodie heard, "Nelson here."

"Hi, Harold. I won't keep you but wanted to let you know we're home. Ann is spending the night and staying until early afternoon tomorrow. Do you want to spend the night here tomorrow?"

"Sure. Will you and Ronnie be alright tomorrow after she leaves? It'll be eleven before I get there."

"Yes. As a matter of fact, I need to be at the office tomorrow by three p.m. I'm taking Ronnie and the dogs with me. We'll go through a drive-through and be home before seven. Sky and Jade can make sure we're fine until you get here."

The last time Jodie and Ann had a sleepover, they were seniors in college. Still chatting at one in the morning, they were surprised when Ronnie came crying and jumped in bed with them. "What's the matter, baby?"

"I have a bad dream again and heard voices. I got scared. I need to sleep here," he said snuggling under the covers between them.

After he fell asleep, Ann asked, "Does he have bad dreams and do this often?"

"Yes and no," was Jodie's answer. "He still occasionally has bad dreams, but this is only the third time he has asked to sleep in my bed."

"Maybe our talking and laughing kept waking him. We'll talk more in the morning. Night."

After breakfast, Jodie started laundry while Ann cleaned the kitchen. Jodie called the Ford dealer and was told they'd have her truck delivered in an hour. She called about her travel trailer and told them she'd pick it up the following morning. After Jodie put in the second load of clothes to wash, they sat on the back porch watching Jade, Sky, and Ronnie play in the yard. Time seemed to fly. Soon it was time for lunch and they ordered Chinese to be delivered. They had time to play two board games with Ronnie, Jade, and Sky on one team and Jodie and Ann on the other. Jodie and Ann lost both games.

After folding and repacking the dry clothes and putting the last load in the dryer, it was time for Ann to leave. Since there was still time before Jodie needed to be at work, she got Ronnie and the dogs into her new truck and went shopping for clothes and a couple of toys and games for Ronnie to play with while they were driving.

After eating their burgers and French fries, they arrived home and Jodie parked the truck in the garage next to the car. Inside the house, she tore off the new tags and packed the clothes. Afterwards, Jodie got the new black fabric and rods she'd bought and took a pair of scissors and the four of them went out to the garage.

Telling Ronnie and the dogs to stay inside the garage where she could see them, she got the ladder and hung the rods and cut material to cover every window. Putting the ladder away, she smiled. No one would be able to see into her locked garage to tell if they were home or not.

With Ronnie bathed and in his pajamas, Jodie read him stories until it was time for bed. After making up the couch for Harold, she turned on the TV and was watching a movie, when there was a knock on the door.

She hadn't heard a car drive up. Sky came running up next to her while Jade stayed with Ronnie. Peeking through window, she saw it was Harold. With a deep sigh, she unlocked the door and let him in while she patted Sky.

"Hi, I didn't hear your car," Jodie said softly so as not to wake Ronnie.

"I parked about a block away, so it might appear that you're alone."

"Thanks, Lieutenant," she tried to act angry. "Are you making us easy targets?"

"Absolutely not," was his rebuff. Grinning he whispered, "Only making it look that way."

"Fine," Jodie pouted. "By the way, you have lipstick on your neck."

"Aw, I thought Ann wiped it off."

"Ann?"

"Yeah, didn't she tell you we were going out tonight?"

"No," Jodie began laughing. "I'm sure she made it a point *not* to tell me."

"Oh, well," he smirked. "Now you know. We've had a few dates. Kissing her is not like kissing a sister."

"Eww! Too much information. I'm going to bed." Jodie giggled all the way.

Jodie woke up with Jade licking her face. "Yuck, go away."

"*Quiet, Jodie. We've got trouble. Get up and go in with Sky and Ronnie and lock the door. I'm going to make sure Lieutenant Harold is awake.*"

Licking Harold's face, Jade jumped back as the Lieutenant came awake, grabbing his pistol from under the pillow and pointing it at the dog.

"Crap! Why'd you do that?" he mumbled.

Jade turned around and took a few steps away and stopped and looked back at him.

"Okay, I've got it," said Harold, following Jade as they quietly walked, with his pistol at his side, toward a window in the kitchen.

Harold and Jade watched as a hand came through a hole cut into the glass and unlocked the window and raise it up. They waited until the intruder was climbing through the open window before the Lieutenant holstered his pistol and rushed forward and pulled him the rest of the way into the kitchen and put handcuffs on one wrist, while pushing him on the floor and pulling his arms around his back and attaching the handcuffs to his other wrist.

"You have the right to remain silent," he began reciting the entire Miranda Rights, as he took a mask off the face of the intruder.

Calling the station, he began, "Officer needs assistance. Everything is under control. It is not an emergency." He gave the address and pulled the intruder to his feet, sitting him on a kitchen chair.

Jade sat watching with a smile on her face, while at the same time growling very softly. She looked very proud of herself.

"What's your name?" the Lieutenant asked.

"I wanna' lawyer." was the reply.

Harold was tempted to say it was a funny name, but he resisted. Instead he said, "Of course you do." He sat down and waited for the sound of police sirens.

The papers and newscasts the next day were full of reports on the arrest of a suspect in the "Cowboy Murders."

EPILOGUE

A year later, Lieutenant Harold Nelson and Ann Wilson were engaged and planning their wedding.

Jodie Pleasant had successfully adopted Ronnie and he had started calling her Mom. She was still pulling the travel trailer behind her truck and calling on several of their company's out-of-state offices.

Jodie's sister, Denise, had started dating a

lawyer that lived near her in St. Louis and announced her time for traveling with Jodie and Ronnie was just about over.

This worked well for Jodie, as Ronnie was excited to be starting kindergarten soon. Jodie had started dating occasionally, and told Ann unless Mr. Right came along, which was doubtful, she was very happy being a single parent.

CAT STORY

"Has it struck you as eerie," Jack sheepishly asked, "that all those deaths from three major accidents have been all around us?"

"No," I snickered looking up from my book. "I hadn't really looked at it that way."

Jack went back to working on his new compound bow, attaching new gadgets to it.

My imagination couldn't fathom shooting arrows from a bow that had peep sights. What will they think of next? Jack always seemed to be buying some new gadget or toy, with which to hunt or fish. I wasn't that surprised at any of his toys anymore, although I tried to take an interest in them.

After smiling at him, I returned to concentrating on the mystery novel I was reading. Still, his statement wouldn't entirely leave me. I wondered where he came up with those weird ideas. Weird ideas or not, I still loved him. The deaths he was referring to were recent and shocking, but to see us in the middle of some sort of accident and death triangle was a good one, even for my husband.

I had stopped reading my book and smiled. I thought about the 25th anniversary we'd celebrated last year. My smile grew larger, proudly thinking about our wonderful family; our son and daughter and Joshua, our two-year old grandson. I'm convinced he is the most beautiful and brilliant little boy that ever existed.

Yawning, my thoughts jumped back to what had been reported on the television. The freezing rain and snow had been the cause of two horrible accidents. Eight people were killed on Highway 55 just north of us, involving two tractor trailers, a school bus, and seven cars.

Jack had driven me to work yesterday and picked me up afterwards, because of the bad road conditions. Highway 55 had still been closed, and it took us two extra hours to get home after work. About the same time as that accident, southwest of us, two people were killed on Highway 270.

I completely gave up reading, remembering the call yesterday morning from my sister Joyce. She was crying and had asked if I'd heard the explosion from the service station, just east of our house. I had heard it, and felt the house tremble, but thought it was a sonic boom.

Joyce works across the street from that station and knew some of the guys which had died. She told me that the window in her office and several others in her building had broken. She asked if our house or others around us received any damage. I assured her that as far as I knew, my neighborhood was fine.

I began thinking about Jack's comment about so many deaths around us. At least fourteen people had been killed yesterday within two miles of where we lived. More might still die. Jack was right. All those deaths did seem to form a triangle around us. Weird!

***

Hearing a noise, my eyes popped wide

open from a sound sleep. Jack was softly snoring beside me. Listening a minute and hearing nothing, I almost dozed off when I heard voices arguing.

"It's not right I tell you," came from a male voice.

"This is the right address," replied a female voice.

"I don't care about the address, this just isn't the right one, trust me"

"Right," was her sarcastic reply.

"She must be near forty-five years old. This takes time and energy and a lot more. I tell you, it's not the right one," the male voice argued.

I realized several things at once. First, they were inside my house. Second, they seemed to be talking about me. Third, instead of fear, I was feeling curious. Fourth, and strangest of all, I realized I wasn't hearing their words at all, I was hearing their thoughts. That was obviously impossible. I decided, I must still be sleeping.

"Oh, oh," came one of their thoughts, "She is awake."

I haven't moved. How could they possibly

know if I'm awake? I don't even know if I'm awake.

"Come in here, lady," coaxed a female voice. No, it was her thought.

My heart is pounding. I should really wake up Jack. I should really be feeling afraid. Yet I feel only curiosity. Something inside of me needed to know how I could hear their thoughts.

I move very quietly, so as not to wake Jack. I slip out of bed, slide my feet into moccasins, grab my robe and creep into the living room.

Naturally, no one was there. Beginning to realize this is some sort of crazy dream, I pinch myself to see if I am even out of bed. I was. Turning around and giggling at my foolishness, I start back to bed.

"Lady, we're over here on the couch," came a voice in my head.

Spinning around, yet thinking this dream was starting to get out of hand, there were two cats on the couch.

"How?" I stammered.

"Sh… sh… sh…" they both thought at the same time, sitting up where they'd been laying, "or you'll wake him."

"But…" I whispered, thinking this is the craziest dream I've ever had. There are two cats in my house that couldn't have possibly gotten in and they're talking, no thinking, to me. Well, I thought, smiling to myself, at least now I know I'm dreaming.

"Please sit down," purred the female cat. "If you have anything to say, just think it. Obviously, we can hear you and you are not dreaming."

"This is serious business," whispered the male cat. "We don't know what to do."

"Phil here thinks it's a mistake, but I disagree because this is the right house. Please sit down while we figure this out."

What could I do? Sitting down in the recliner, I knew this was the weirdest dream I'd ever had. Since I'm dreaming, what harm can it do to sit and talk to these cats. I can hardly wait to tell Jack about this dream in the morning.

The cats didn't give me time for thinking, as they were chatting a mile a minute. I was only catching bits and pieces of what they were saying, rather thinking.

Looking at the white spot on her ear, I

heard the female cat say to Phil, "I don't believe she could understand us if she wasn't the right one."

"You don't know that for a fact," was his reply.

"Look, all we're supposed to do is carry out the orders, not question them," she scolded.

"I still think someone goofed," was his comeback. "And besides, once we explain her duties, what will we do if she doesn't cooperate?" Phil sounded as though he was losing patience.

Even though I knew this was a silly dream, my curiosity continued to build. Could what I'd eaten for dinner have caused this? Feeling impatient myself, while thinking about that pretty white spot on her ear, I was about to interrupt their discussion.

"My name is Penelope; Penny for short. This is my partner, Phil. Thanks for admiring my ear. I'm fond of that white spot myself. Listen up, Jean. May I call you Jean?" Without waiting for permission, she continued. "The last human we worked with went bonkers, so we're at this address looking for you, I guess. The deliveries are supposed to be sent to this address. Phil here, says you're too old. Does anyone else live here besides you and Jack?"

"Our son is twenty-two and has his room downstairs," was my quick reply.

Penny's disappointment was obvious when she said, "No, it's got to be a female this time. You see, last time it was a man. It always rotates."

Turning to Phil, feeling relieved I said, "I'm terribly sorry, Phil. You're probably right. This is all a mistake. I'd like to get back to bed so I can wake up. I have a big day at work tomorrow. I'm training a new secretary and need my sleep. After all," I smirked, "I'm pretty old."

"There, see what you've gone and done Phil," Penny spat, swinging her paw at Phil. "You've upset her. Jean darling, don't pay any attention to Phil. He can be quite nice when you get to know him. He tends to be very precise and his concern is that you are slightly older than the others. He just wants to be sure."

Penny jumped off the couch and up on my lap, smiling at me. Of course, I'm just dreaming, so why couldn't cats smile in dreams.

"Jean darling, do you mind if I sit on your lap? This is going to take a while so we might as well be comfortable."

"Humpf," came a sound from Phil.

"Since all you have to do is listen," Penny continued. "Would you just scratch a little behind my ears? Very gentle now, that-a-way, and you may also stroke my back. Ah yes, that feels good."

"Humpf," came from Phil again.

"We'll begin by giving the ring to you. Phil, please come over by us and give Jean the ring."

"I don't know, Penny."

"Phil," she shouted although it was still just in my mind. "The ring!"

Slowly Phil walked down the length of the couch, jumped down and leaped into my lap right next to Penny. He took a ring on a silk thread from around his neck and placed it in my hand. "I'll bet it won't fit."

"Let's try it on," suggested Penny. Placing it on the ring finger of my right hand, it fit perfectly.

"There," purred Penny. "That proves it once

and for all."

"Humpf" growled Phil, sitting down where he was on my lap next to Penny.

Starring, it certainly wasn't the most beautiful ring I'd ever seen. In fact, it was rather plain and unremarkable. It appeared to be made of wood. Hope it's stronger than it looks or it'll break if I'm to wear it. How strange! But this is obviously a strange dream anyway.

Absently, I dropped a hand on each cat and began stroking them lightly, while Penny continued. "First, I must ask, do you believe in God and the devil?"

"Of course," I said. "But I don't recall ever being asked if I believe in the devil. I trust and believe that God will take me to Heaven when I die. I know the devil exists, but I don't want any part of him."

"Good," Penny went on, "that's fine. Now, you see, I'm not able to explain all of God's ways in dealing with the devil. But because of the devil, death exists. That's not all bad, because when some people die, they go to Heaven."

"Give it to her straight, Pen," Phil

interrupted. "Some people that die belong to God and some belong to the devil. It's not for us to decide who belongs to whom. That's up to God. Our job here is to explain what will concern you when they die."

"Okay, okay, Phil, let's back up. Jean has stopped scratching my ears and her eyes are enlarged and she thinks her dream is going into a nightmare."

"How do you do that," I snapped. "Of course," I sighed. "You can read my mind."

"Relax," purred Penny.

I began to like her purring.

"We're going to explain," Phil began. "Death is sort of an arrangement between God and the devil. God has limited the number of deaths for the devil and he can't go over that number in any one area. The way I think it works, is that some human is in charge of a certain area. Your area runs about nine miles in all four directions from your house. Some people have smaller and some have larger areas. It seems to depend on several things, like population, or how hard it is to travel within their area."

I whisper feeling confused, "Are you trying

to convince me that I have something to do with the death of everyone inside this nine-mile square or circle?"

"Yes and no," was his reply. "Let us explain further. You don't pick which ones die. God does that. But you have to sort them out, so they go to the right place."

"Your ring," Penny spoke up, "is like a computer that does the actual sorting. You just have to get close enough for it to classify them and send their soul to the right place. This means, you can't take long vacations and then try to make up the lost time, for all the deaths like one human did. You have to keep up. That guy got behind and tried to do too many in one day. We don't know what happened exactly. I think the devil did a slow burn trying to handle too many in one day for that area. Some areas can probably handle thousands or millions in a day, but it has to be set up for it."

"Penny, hurry up, we don't have all night. That guy's ring burned out, like a computer overload. It was his turn to be replaced soon anyway. It's not a lifetime job. So, another human was found for that area. At any rate, the average number for this area is twenty-five per quarter. There is only seven more days before this quarter ends. Because of the 20 tragedies yesterday, they need to be sorted right away. It is actually possible for the number to be over or under 25 deaths in this area, as long as the list is kept up to date. So far, no one else has died here this morning, but yesterday twenty people died. Before five more die within the next seven days, yesterday's twenty need to be sorted. You are evidently the new one selected for this area, and you will need to get started right away."

Penny jumped back in. "Part of the rush is our fault. We got behind searching for the right person for this area because the first two we tried refused. We were then sent your address and here we are. Do you have any questions Jean? You're beginning to look a little glassy eyed."

"Uh, yea! I thought fourteen died yesterday."

"Nah!" Phil began. "Those 14 were only the close ones you heard about. The other six were due to natural causes."

"Okay," I began, trying to understand them.

"Let me see if I've got this right. I have a quota of about 25 deaths every three months for this nine-mile square area. The names are pre-selected, and somehow I have to get close enough to them so the ring can pull the score card on their life, file them into its computer so they're sent to Heaven or Hell, depending to whom they belong."

"There," Penny was beaming. "What did I tell you Phil? That's very good, Jean. It's a very good, simplified way of putting it."

"Thanks," I said trying not to yawn. "May I go to bed now so I can wake up? I've got a big day tomorrow."

"Su... sure," Penny stuttered. "Go right on to bed."

They both jumped down from my lap. As I was walking back to the bedroom, I heard Phil whisper, "Nincompoop! She doesn't understand at all. Why'd you let her go? She still thinks she's dreaming."

"I know. We'll talk to her again tomorrow. Besides, how is she going to explain our presence to Jack, if we have just been a part of her dream? I'm tired Phil," she yawned. "Where shall we sleep? Jean didn't say."

"That couch looks fine to me," Phil growled. "I'm not tired though, I'm worried about her. I still say someone made a mistake and she is not the right one."

***

"Jack," I moaned. "The alarm's going off."

"Uh huh."

"Jack!"

"Oh, alright. How come I have to turn off the alarm and how come I have to turn up the heat when it's cold?"

"Because the clock is on your side of the bed and because it's too cold for me."

"Not fair! It's also cold for me and besides you should get up first because you take so much longer to get ready. So, you should turn off the alarm and turn up the heat."

"We've been over and over this Jack. It's too cold for me and the clock is on your side."

Slowly, coming back into the bedroom, Jack began, "Uh Jean, when I turned up the heat just now, I noticed two cats sleeping on the couch. Where'd they come from? Do you think JJ brought them home? If so, they should be down in his room."

"Cats!" I exclaimed.

"Two of them," Jack repeated.

"Oh noooooo!" I felt suddenly very faint. "Jack what time is it?"

"6:10 a.m."

"Are we defiantly awake?"

"Of course we're awake."

"And there are two cats on our couch?"

"Yes, get up and come see them for yourself if you don't believe me," Jack pouted.

"Uh uh! I don't want to. I'm too old."

"What!" Jack raised his voice. "Jean, are you alright?"

"I don't think so. Jack, last night you mentioned something about us being in a triangle with death all around us."

"Huh?"

"Remember, you said that about those fourteen deaths all around us yesterday?"

"Oh that. I just thought that it was weird to have so many deaths so close to us."

"Yeah, actually there were twenty deaths here in our area yesterday and it's not a triangle, it's a square."

"Really, how do you know? Did you hear something on the radio or TV? Were there more that died from the accidents?"

"No, don't know for sure how the others died. Might have been natural causes."

"Then how do you know?

"Well uh, the cats told me."

"Jean, that's not funny. Now, unless you're really sick, get up and get going. I don't want to be late."

"The cats were just part of my dream."

"Enough about the cats," he sneered. "JJ probably brought them home. We'll ask him later. "Up, up, up."

"Okay, I'm going, but —"

"Go, go, go."

Very slowly I walked past him, glancing at the couch in the living room. "Hi," purred Penny.

"What's for breakfast?" growled Phil.

I shook my head, walked back to the bathroom and began running water in the tub.

It can't be, I kept saying to myself, over and over. *It just can't be. There's a logical explanation for all of this. I'm probably going crazy. Maybe I've been working too hard. Maybe I need a vacation. But the cats said I can't take a long vacation because I'm already behind on my quota.*

What was I thinking? There's got to be a logical explanation. I sank down into the warm suds and pushed all thoughts from my mind except the bliss of warm water all over my body.

"Jean! It's 6:30, what are you doing in there?"

I quickly scrubbed my body and washed and rinsed my hair. After drying off I began fixing a hasty breakfast and then rushed back to the bedroom to get dressed. I hadn't closed the door and saw Phil standing in the doorway eyeing me warily. "You are going to feed us, aren't you?"

"Huh, oh sure," I mumbled.

"Who are you talking to?" came from Jack.

"Just one of the cats," I replied. "He's hungry. We don't have any cat food. I'll just fry a couple more eggs."

"Okay, but hurry! We're late and let's not forget to ask JJ where the cats came from."

The ride to work was quiet. Jack was pouting and I think I fell asleep until he stopped the car to let me out at work. We kissed, said goodbye, and I rushed in to work.

Training a new girl takes almost full

concentration, but there were moments when I couldn't push last night from my thoughts. Even though I work twelve miles from our home, I thought I could almost hear those darn cats trying to talk to me.

What's wrong with me? One day I'm fine and the next day, I'm bonkers. What would Jack do without me if I go whacky? He's just a big kid. He needs me. What about our divorced daughter Jodie and Joshua, our grandson. They need me. This can't happen to me.

Suddenly I got it. I'll pray. There's just a little slip in my wires; nothing serious. I'll pray just as soon as I get home. I called JJ but he insisted he hadn't brought any cats home. Jack had seen the cats, so they were real. Where did they come from?

Ah hah! My sister Joyce; the practical joker. She has keys to our house. She knows we like animals and she probably came by late and put them inside and left. Boy, I'll get her for this one.

"Jean," my secretary trainee began, "I'm sorry, but I don't remember if I'm supposed to line the type up with the logo or the name of the company."

"With the logo, honey."

"Okay thanks, like this?"

"Right, that's very good."

I was too busy to think about the cats the rest of the day. Suddenly it was 5:15 p.m. and Jack was there to pick me up.

"How was your day, honey?" Jack asked watching me get into the car.

"Busy, hardly had time to go potty," I smiled. "How about yours?"

"Yeah, mine was busy too. I'm training a guy to operate one of the new computers."

"Guess what. I called JJ and he didn't bring the cats home, but I think Joyce might have done it."

"I thought you said you dreamed them up."

"Did I? I think the cats must have been in my dreams, but I bet anything that Joyce did it. She's laughing her guts out about it right now."

"Could be, could be. What's for dinner? I have to leave by 6:30 p.m. because it's my turn to drive the guys to the archery range. I can't wait to try out my new sights."

"Gee, I wish you didn't have to go tonight."

"Honey, I go every Thursday. It's the only thing I do."

Right I thought, besides your many long weekends to fish or hunt.

"I don't bowl, smoke, or drink," he continued. "Surely you don't begrudge me this one night out."

"But tonight," I whined. "I… I just… those cats and everything."

"I'll be home by 10:00 p.m. We'll talk about what to do with them then. I hate to think about taking them to the pound. Full grown cats don't find homes too easy. But we'll talk about it later."

I pouted the rest of the way home and Jack pretended he was concentrating on his driving.

Jack unlocked the door and held it open for me. Feeling crabby, I asked myself why gentlemen held the door open for ladies to go in first. Real gentlemen should go in first to make sure it was safe inside. Anything could be lurking inside to pounce on the first one through the doors. But no, Jack held open the door and I had to go in first. I decided that all men are cowards. They started this propaganda that it's the gentlemanly thing to hold the door while all the time they're stinking cowards.

Hummmm. So far so good. Jack is right behind me. He has stopped to read the mail. Should I wait by him until he's finished? I've got to go to the bathroom; might as well get this over with.

No sign of the cats so far. They'll probably wait until I pull my pants down and start to sit and then they'll jump out at me. Yuck! I'm not afraid of cats. What's going on? I'm losing my mind. That's what it is and probably because I forgot to pray. Off the pot with hands washed, no cats in sight and I'm ready to start supper. Jack, bless his cowardly heart is still reading the mail. What's taking him so long? Is he waiting for me to check all the other rooms to be sure it's safe to move?

The cats are probably in the kitchen waiting for something to eat. We forgot to stop for cat food; besides there wasn't time. Why should we buy cat food if we're not keeping them? They can have part of our hamburgers tonight.

Well, they are not in the kitchen either.

Joyce probably came and got them and she is still laughing about it. Maybe my mind hasn't flipped after all. It was just Joyce and dreams and I didn't even have to pray. Thanks God. You answered that one before I even prayed.

"What are you humming and acting so cheerful about?" Jack questioned as he came into the kitchen slipping his arms around me. "Planning on your boyfriend coming over while I'm out?"

"Right," I sassed back turning around and kissing him on his somewhat longish nose. "I have him over every Thursday from 7:00 p.m. until 9:00 p.m."

"Is he as good at it as I am?" he nuzzled my neck.

"At what: archery shooting?" I teased.

"You know," Jack whispers. "Maybe I should take you in the bedroom now and get you warmed up for him."

"Your choice. You can have dinner or romance but you can't have both by 6:30. Now if you don't take your hands off me and start helping, you might not get either."

Jack pretended to be hurt as he got down the plates and glasses. "Is JJ coming home for dinner tonight?"

"No, when I talked to him from the office, he said he had to work late. It'll just be the two of us. Sure you have to go tonight? We could make this a humdinger of an evening."

"Oh, you wanton woman," he laughed. "Act your age. Is that all you ever think about?"

"Me! You started this with your lewd suggestions earlier."

"That's right, blame me," he teased. "I get blamed for everything. Aren't those hamburgers done yet, I'm starved."

After dinner and dishes, Jack rounded up all his archery paraphernalia and it was exactly 6:30 p.m. Kissing me on the mouth, he rushes out the door.

After putting on my nightgown and brushing me teeth, I climbed into bed to read, but I couldn't find my glasses.

"They're on the floor," Phil says.

I reach down, pick them up and say thanks. I'm putting them on when it sinks in. "Oh no, you're back." Darn I think, *I should have prayed.*

"Look," begins Penny hopping up on the bed next to Phil. "We're sorry you're unhappy to have us but you'll get used to us. You'd be surprised at how many other people have cats that communicate with them. You're really quite fortunate because we are very wonderful cats."

"No, no. I am not sleeping yet. How can I be dreaming? This means I really am losing my mind."

Penny moves closer and pats my head as I start to cry. "There, there, it's really not as bad as all that. Scratch my ears and stroke my back and it'll take you mind off your troubles. Phil, come here. The first thing we have to do is convince Jean she isn't crazy. It has now been two days since no one has died and that's great. But we can't afford to get any further behind."

"No," I continue to wail.

"I think maybe she really is bonkers," Phil says nastily.

I stop crying long enough to look up and cast him a killing stare.

"Phil, that wasn't nice. Tell Jean you're sorry."

"Yeah, well, anyone in their right mind would know they weren't dreaming and weren't crazy, when they saw the ring on their finger was real."

The ring! Sure enough there it was. How come no one at work had noticed it? Someone usually notices things like that.

"The ring really exists. That proves you really talk to me, and Joyce didn't drop you off, and I've really got to be involved in the deaths in this area."

"That's right and you're not bonkers," smirked Phil turning to Penny. "Okay, that's the first thing accomplished. What's next?"

"The easiest way for her to begin is to just begin. Jack is not home and neither is JJ, so we might as well do one now. Then she won't be frightened of the unknown. She'll see how easy it is."

"Gotcha'," Phil snaps, jumping down and running out the bedroom door.

"Come on, honey," coaxed Penny. "Get dressed and let's do one and get it over with. I'll get the list."

"Let's don't forget to buy cat food and milk while we're out," pleaded Phil.

Penny shows her a long list of names. "We need to do all of these?" I question looking at names and addresses, most of which are addresses of funeral homes.

"Fraid so, my friend," purrs Penny.

"Put your coat on and make sure you have a map," Phil orders.

"Penny," I ask. "Do we start at the top or choose one closest to us?"

"Let's take the closest," she decides.

"Okay, I recognize most of these funeral homes. This one is the closest. The name on the list is Ralph Parker. I don't know him."

"That's fine," says Phil reaching a paw up to me. "Take one of Penny's paws and one of mine and a deep breath."

ZAP was the only sound I heard as I felt a flash of warmth. Blinking my eyes open, we were standing outside a funeral home that was less than a mile away from our house.

"Turn loose," hissed Phil. I released both their paws.

Now what, I wondered and glanced down at my right hand. The ring had turned silver for about ten seconds and then it turned white and then it was back to its look of brownish wood.

"Cross him off our list," was Phil's

response. "That one went to Heaven."

"That's it," I could hardly believe it.

"That's it honey," came from Penny. "Let's do another."

"William Butler is close by. Let's do him next," I said.

Taking their paws again caused another ZAP.

Standing in the parking lot of this funeral home, I looked at the ring. Once again it turned silver for about ten seconds, but then it turned red and then back to brown.

"Aw," groaned Penny. "That one belonged to the devil."

This time I felt extremely sad. "I don't know why, but somehow I feel a little guilty."

Penny jumped up and I caught her in my arms. She licked my cheek and said, "Silly girl, it's not your fault he belonged to the devil."

Sounding a little subdued Phil suggested we do one more and then go buy cat food. That one turned white, which left me feeling a little better.

Taking their paws again, with the ZAP we were back home. They scrambled into the car and we drove to the store. The cats stayed while I went in and bought two small bags of cat kibble, a variety of canned food, three cat bowls, and a gallon of milk.

As soon as we arrived back home, I poured water into one of the bowls and put some kibble into one of the others. Then I opened one of the cans explaining to the cats that I didn't know what foods they preferred. Between mouths full of food, they assured me they were not picky, but Phil added that he was glad I hadn't purchased the cheap stuff.

"Look," I said to them turning to go sit on the couch. "When you two are finished eating, I've got some questions."

Shortly both of them joined me on the couch and began grooming themselves, looking just like ordinary cats.

"Why do God and the devil do it this way?" I began. "Why couldn't you two handle this area with the ring around your neck? I'd like to know more about the people that are getting sorted by this ring."

"Jean, we don't know the answers to your first two questions," was Penny's soft reply. "As far as finding out more about the dead people, you could probably find out a little bit about them from the obituaries in the paper or look for their name in the telephone book."

Finishing grooming herself, Penny curled up in my lap and rubbed her head against my hand. "Ah, that's good. Now a couple of strokes down my back and then of course repeat."

While I did as she asked, she continued explaining more of the situation. "Once a day about this time in the evening, we often find the names and addresses on a piece of paper about a foot away from one of us. Don't know how it gets there. Occasionally there is a name on the list that hasn't died yet."

"An interesting thing about the list is that sometimes the address of the deceased person on the list changes. Usually that's because before the human visits them, they've already been buried or cremated, so the address changes." Penny finished.

"Wait! You mean this ring works even after they've been cremated?"

"Of course," Phil piped in. "What about all the people that are blown to pieces like what just happened at the service station or when a house burns down or they drown and fish eat them."

My face drained of color and I thought I might have to run to the bathroom.

"We don't know the how or why to most of it," Penny spoke up. "Please continue with scratching my ears. Thanks. Perhaps it is done differently in other areas, but this is just the way it's done here. Our job is to give you the list and provide transportation for you when you need it. That's basically all I know."

Phil stood up and starred in my eyes. "Jack won't be home for at least an hour. Shall we do another name or two?"

Without answering, I grabbed my coat while looking at a name and said, "Joseph LaGrange." The cats took my hand and ZAP, we were at another funeral home. The ring turned white and I drew a sigh of relief. Next, we chose Peter Felton at a crematory. It also turned white. Those two went so fast, we did two more; one of which turned red. Then we ZAPPED back home and I collapsed in my rocking chair.

"Six was good for your first evening at this," Phil's voice in my head actually sounded more pleasant than usual. "However, there are still fifteen more to go and not many days left in this quarter."

"No," I argued. "Six from twenty is fourteen, not fifteen."

"Sorry," Phil responded. "See this paper that just arrived at my feet. There has been one new death today here in your area; a Rhoda Southers."

"I'm beat," I moaned. "Can't handle any more of this; going to bed early. Oh, I just thought, do either of you need for me to get you a box of sand or anything?"

"No thanks," came the thought from Penny. "We do our business outside or in the toilet; we know how to flush. Good night."

"Wait!" said Phil, "I suggest we meet you at your office tomorrow at noon, so we can handle a couple of these names on your lunch hour."

With a heavy sigh, I nodded. "Meet you out in back of the building at 12:00 noon."

***

Jumping up and running around the bed to

turn off the alarm clock, I ran to the bathroom to shower and brush my teeth. When finished, jamming my bathrobe closed, I rounded the bed and shook Jack awake. "Hey sleepy head, I'm headed to the kitchen to fix fried potatoes and eggs. Roads are fine today with no bad weather predicted, so I'm driving myself. I may be a few minutes late coming home."

"Okay," he mumbled trying to get up while I rushed to the kitchen, refreshing the water bowl for the cats and giving them more kibble. I'd open a can for them tonight.

When the cats slowly went to eat some of the kibble, I told them, "I'm driving myself to work today and thought we'd get a couple more names crossed off the list on the way home."

"Good idea," came a weak response from Phil. "Uh, would you fry an extra egg for Penny and me to split?"

Looking at Penny for confirmation, I swear she smiled at me. "No problem," I said while I continued making breakfast.

***

On my lunch hour, we were able to cross off four more names. Eleven more to go. My afternoon at work went well as the new secretary was finally starting to understand her duties. Crossing off three more names on the way home, I was feeling elated with only eight more to go. We still got home before Jack, so I opened a can of food for the cats and began boiling water for the pasta and getting the fish ready to bake.

"Ooooh," Phil muttered from a kitchen chair. "I love fish."

Turning on him with a spoon in my hand, I yelled a threat, "You touch that fish and you are a dead cat, mister."

"Whoa sweetheart," he sounded serious. "I know my place and can wait for left-overs, but if you should want to cut off a small tidbit while it's raw, I wouldn't object."

"Oh, alright," I relented. "A very small piece for each of you." They pounced eagerly on their raw fish and then sat back and licked their paws. I'd have to remember to get extra fish next time.

After giving the cats the left-over bits of fish after dinner, Jack and I cleaned up the kitchen, then went to the living room to listen to the news. The local news spoke of a death in the city that was probably gang related and I sighed, feeling relieved. It wasn't in my area.

Looking down at Phil by my feet, I saw the piece of paper he was looking at; another female death in my area. That put my remaining deaths from eight up to nine. I slumped back on the couch.

"Honey," Jack spoke. "It's early but I'm going to read in bed and hopefully fall asleep. It was another rough day training a slow learner and still trying to get my own work finished. Hope the girl you are training is learning faster than my guy."

"She is," I smiled, kissing his cheek. "I'll keep the television low and try not to wake you when I come to bed. It's nice out tonight. I might take a walk."

"Fine," was what I think he said in a low voice.

"Okay kids," I whispered when I heard the bedroom door close. "Let's go for a walk."

Climbing quietly into bed later, having crossed two more names off the list, the number seven kept running through my mind.

Only seven more to clear off the rest of those names. This still felt crazy to me, but it shouldn't be too much trouble after I got this list cleared. I saw little 'sevens' running in my mind as I drifted off to sleep.

***

One Year Later

Speaking verbally to the cats I said, "Cindy Mason, this new name on the list hasn't died yet. I'll call her when I get to work and try to see her."

"Jack just heard you say that," Phil's thought came to me.

Turning to face Jack, my face turned beet red and I couldn't speak.

"Who is Cindy Mason?" Jack asked.

I couldn't lie to Jack, I never have. Of course, I hadn't told him about the 'death list' and my part of it either, so I knew that was lying by omission.

"Jack," I began. "If I explain now we are going to be very late to work or I can explain this evening."

Jack didn't say anything for a minute. "I haven't been late to work for ages. I think I will be today. Let me call and let them know. Maybe you should call in too." He reached for his cell phone and started making the call.

The home phone was within reach, so I called in, leaving a message that I'd be late.

Putting his phone away, Jack took my hand and sat down next to me. "Go ahead."

I looked at the cats. "Go for it," Penny sent to me. "There have been a few other couples that did this as a team."

"I didn't know that was possible," I snarled at her.

"I'm waiting," Jack said patiently.

"Okay, you probably won't believe me or will think I'm crazy, but here goes. I'll start by telling you Phil and Penny are not normal cats. They can read my mind and I understand their thoughts also."

Jack said nothing; he just frowned.

I sent a quick thought to the cats. "Can you send a thought to Jack so he believes that much?"

"We can try and see if it works. Hi Jack,"

sent Phil. "How are you this morning?" sent Penny.

"Holy sh…" was Jack's shocked response.

"Good," I said out loud. "That should make this a little easier." The cats and I took turns explaining about the 'death list' and the 'ring' and the ZAP transportation.

"How long has this been going on?" Jack's voice sounded like he was in shock.

"For me it has been a year," I answered.

Phil said, "A lot longer for us."

"There is a little more," I suggested sheepishly.

"Tell me," he said.

"More and more names started showing up on the 'death list' that were not yet dead and often didn't die for four or five days. Their home and cell telephone numbers were usually included on the list, so I began immediately praying for them. Then I decided to take it a step farther and contacted them, asking to see them immediately. Many refused, but before they hung up I'd tell them I was praying for them. It was probably rude of me, but a few times I showed up at their house, knocked on their door and if an adult answered I told them that they or their spouse was going to die very soon. I often got the door slammed in my face. But I felt a sense of peace that I had tried. I thought God wanted me to try."

"A few of those I contacted on the phone actually agreed to see me since I told them it was something very urgent about them or their spouse. Some invited me to their home. Others preferred to meet me in a public place such as the library or a restaurant. I figured I'd only get that one chance to see and talk to them, so I wasted very little time getting to the point."

"I usually started by telling them they would have a hard time believing me and beg them to please just hear me out. I hinted at being psychic and assured them I wanted nothing from them. If one of them was seriously ill, they tended to believe me when I told them they are going to die very soon. Still some would laugh at me and some yelled for me to leave them alone. One lady shoved me so hard I fell down. Some continued to think I wanted money from them. Gradually, I stopped trying to see or talk to them."

"Occasionally, I still call to see if they are available to see me. But I no longer tell them about one of them dying, I just leave a Christian tract and tell them God loves them and I'll be praying for them. I doubt my efforts have led any of the unbelievers to have an immediate conversion to faith in God. But Jack, I'm doing what I think God has called me to do."

I speak out loud to the cats, "Remember the ring went red when George Minks died. His wife, Glenda died about six months later and the ring was white for her. I know that doesn't prove anything, but it gives me hope."

Jack just sat there slowly shaking his head while still holding my hand. "I believe you darling. It's just that this is all so bazaar. I can't believe you've been doing this for a year without my knowing; without telling me. Why didn't you tell me? Were you afraid I wouldn't believe you or try to stop you? I am having more trouble understanding why you didn't tell me, than I am with this whole situation."

"Oh honey! I'm so sorry. Will you please forgive me? I love you so much and don't want you to be angry. If this bothers you, I promise I'll quit."

"I love you too, Jean. Of course, I forgive you and I'm not angry. I think I need a little time to adjust to everything you've told me. In fact, I don't think I want to go to work today. I'm going to take a personal day off. How about you? What do you think about us going to the zoo or doing something fun together?"

"Sounds wonderful," I grinned as I kissed him hard on the mouth. The cats wisely say nothing.

The next evening Jack went with me and the cats to a funeral home near our house. We didn't go inside but watched as the ring turned white. "Is this all you have to do?"

The cats said "Yes" to Jack so I didn't need to answer.

"Now is it possible for me to go with the cats without you, Jean?"

"I don't know."

"Give Jack the ring and let's try," mewed Penny. But nothing happened.

After giving me back the ring, the four of us next went to a cemetery. That one turned red.

"That is depressing," was Jack's only

response. "I can't understand why this is necessary."

"We don't either," I murmured, putting my arms around Jack. "However, I believe the ring has turned white much more than it did at first. I believe it's because God can use my slight contact with them, to bring them or their spouse to faith."

"Well, that sounds very humbling to think that our God is using you that way. I think I'd like to go with you on one of those calls."

"Okay, let's call on Cindy Mason tomorrow evening. Bear in mind that we don't know where she is in her faith walk and even when we part company, we won't know if what we say will make any difference."

"Agreed," was Jack's only reply.

***

Six Months Later

I cuddled up next to Jack on the couch, with Phil and Penny by my feet. "What shall we do this weekend? There are no more names on the list and a new list hasn't arrived."

Before Jack has a chance to answer, Phil smiles up at us. "Jean and Jack, we're leaving tonight and we need the ring."

"Phil, don't be so crude. Let me explain," Penny went on. "A new person has been chosen for this area. Your time is over."

"Why?" I asked softly. "Was I not up to God's standard, or is one of us going to die soon? I don't understand."

Penny patted my arm giving me her special smile. "Jean, my dear, your work was excellent and as far as I know, neither of you are due to die soon."

"That's just the way God does it," Phil jumped in. "We don't question it. He rules."

"Of course, He rules," I snapped back.

Jack squeezed my shoulder. "Jean darling, we'll pray about it, but God is in charge and I don't want us to question His decision on this. Okay?"

"Sure," I slump closer to Jack, remove the ring and hand it to Penny.

Nora Jean Broleman was born and raised in Missouri. She and Jack, her husband of over 60 years, live on a farm in mid-Missouri, with lots of critters. Thanks to their daughter and son, they have one daughter-in-law, one son-in-law, one granddaughter, three grandsons, three granddaughters-in-law, and three great-grandchildren.

The Brolemans currently have dogs, cats, chickens, ducks, geese, guinea, peacocks, and a crested gecko. Over the years, they have raised many different kinds of animals, including buffalo, goats, coatimundi, kangaroo, and black swans.

Jean is active in two writing groups. She credits them for helping in her writing. Her first published book is *Jeannie 'Outta This World*. She also has published the short story *Olive's Old Pink Hog*.